How to Not Tell a War Story

Michael Lund

BeachhouseBooks

Chesterfield Missouri USA

How to Not Tell a War Story,

Copyright 2012 Michael Lund

Cover Design by John Lund

"How to Not Tell a War Story" was previously published in *War, Literature & the Arts: an international journal of the humanities*, Volume 24, 2012.

ISBN9781596300798 beachhousebooks.com/

The Smashwords Electronic Edition Is simultaneously Published by MilSpeak Books A Division of MilSpeak Foundation, Inc. (501c3) http://www.milspeak.org

BeachHouse Books

www.beachhousebooks.com

an Imprint of
Science & Humanities Press
PO Box 7151
Chesterfield, MO 63006-7151
(636) 394-4950

For Soldiers and Those Who Care for Them

As Mr. Brent remarks (5/16 'Journal of Horticulture' October 22, 1861 p. 76),: "Every few seconds over they [common English tumbling pigeons] go; one, two, or three somersaults at a time. Here and there a bird gives a very quick and rapid spin, revolving like a wheel, though they sometimes lose their balance and make a rather ungraceful fall . . .

—Charles Darwin, The Variation of Animals and Plants Under Domestication, 1868

. . . said Wemmick. "By-the-bye; you were quite a pigeon-fancier." The man looked up at the sky. "I am told you had a remarkable breed of tumblers. Could you commission any friend of yours to bring me a pair, if you've no further use for 'em?"

—Charles Dickens, *Great Expectations*

. . . going to war, whether you're the one on the frontline or the homefront, is like going to Mars, and living here with the Martians, and hearing only Martianese being spoken. . . . And then one day you go back to Earth, maybe just for a visit, maybe for good, and as you step off the spaceship, all around you in the spaceport you hear a Babel of voices, over the loudspeaker, passing you in the concourse, speaking in some strange foreign tongue, and all of a sudden, it hits you — that's the language you grew up speaking.

—Kristin Henderson, While They're at War: The True Story of American Families on the Homefront

Acknowledgments

Portions of two stories originally appeared in *Route 66 to Vietnam: A Draftee's Story* (2004 BeachHouse Books). "How to Not Tell a War Story" appeared, in a slightly different form, in *War, Literature, and the Arts* (2012); and "Exchange" was first seen in *MilSpeak Memo* (March 2012). We are grateful for permission to reprint this material here.

My thanks to Bud Banis at BeachHouse Books and to Sally Drumm at MilSpeak Books (which is publishing an electronic version of this volume) for understanding what led me to write these stories and for judging them worthy. Bill Frank, Geoffrey Orth, Susan Robins, and Willie Smith, Jr. offered timely suggestions during composition, and the collection is better because of them. Any errors or oversights, of course, are entirely the fault of the author.

I would not have survived the experiences that inspired these stories or the years since without the love of my wife, Anne. If there are models for kindness in this work, they come from her.

Table of Contents

Acknowledgments 5

Author's Preface: Coming Home........................1

How to Not Tell a War Story 10

The Ugly Sweater Holiday Party 23

Writing in the Sand 37

The Midnight Chopper 51

Who Do You Think Were There?.....................71

Fountain..88

Jody 120

Re-up...141

The Clean Plate Club 161

Exchange 180

Tumbling Pigeons 195

Reunion 209

The Concrete Boat 234

Boiling Lobster on the Fourth of July............255

Author's Epilogue: Going 278

About the Author...286

Credits...287

Author's Preface: Coming Home

Forty-some years ago a friend drove my wife to New Jersey so that she could meet me when I returned from Vietnam. They had been teaching school together that year in Virginia. Another friend, resuming her interrupted college career, had shared an apartment with my wife in the months that I was gone. Those two women assumed a role that many did in that difficult period of American history: helping military families cope with separation. This book is in part an appreciation of their kindness and an exploration of models we need to follow with more commitment in the era of a volunteer military.

Though I didn't realize it at the time, I began composing this study of the Vietnam War then and of veterans' families later one early summer evening about twenty-five years ago. At a church vestry meeting, after the minister had offered an opening prayer that God direct and bless our actions, one senior member added, "And remember those boys who gave their lives this day forty years ago." It was the anniversary of D-Day.

Eager to finish the meeting, get home to my wife and children, and continue preparations for the work day in the morning, I thought to myself, "What's the matter with you, old-timer? WWII is ancient history! Get over it." And silently I renewed a vow I'd already made: never to become one of those tiresome veterans who can't move on, who find the rest of their lives insignificant compared to the intensity of that one experience.

I have, in general, been true to that commitment, valuing the accomplishments of my personal and (civilian) professional life far more than my very brief military career. However, in recent years I have also found myself drawn back in memory and imagination to my time in Vietnam. The stories that follow — all fictional, but inspired by real events — are one result of my inability completely to "get over it." And, among other things, they are an apology to my fellow church member, now deceased, who prayed for his friends.

My conviction not to remain stuck in the past was officially adopted one day in Princeton, New Jersey, spring, 1971. I was standing beside an open grave into which the body of a young soldier killed in Vietnam was about to be lowered. Stephen Warner's mother, his father, his younger sister, and family friends watched as military personnel (I was one member of that escort team) removed the flag from the casket, folded the Stars and Stripes in the honored triangular fashion, and handed it to his mother.

I had been with the Warner family for several days, and I believed this would be my last act in a drama I had been caught up in two years earlier. When the ceremony at the gravesite and a small family gathering afterward were concluded, I would go to a local motel where my wife, (having arrived with her colleague from work the day before) would meet me. Within days I would become again a civilian, having put to rest (may they rest in peace!) the pains and pleasures of service.

I had never anticipated having a military life; so I saw my two-year stint as a break in a planned civilian career. I didn't realize for some decades that being in the service is not something you can edit out of your personal history. The military stays in you and you in the military, no matter how short that time.

Stephen Warner had been, like me, a draftee. He had completed his undergraduate education at Gettysburg College in Pennsylvania and gone on to his first year of law school at Yale, committed to the civil rights movement in this country and opposed to the war overseas. The Army selected him, as it had me, to be a correspondent; and he discovered, after he arrived in-country, an unanticipated mission. He would tell the story of the infantry, the "grunts." Armed with his notepad, pen, and camera, he began, as it was termed, "humping the boonies" and recording what he learned. Now, unexpectedly, I find myself attempting to put into words the thoughts and feelings of my fellow soldiers.

One of those ironies of conflict you don't believe when you hear about it is true in his case: he had orders to go home before the last mission

3

that took his life. He turned down the "early out," offered as part of an accelerated drawdown which President Nixon had mandated, in order to accompany one more time the unit he had gotten to know and whose story he was determined to preserve in word and picture. Traveling with that infantry platoon headed north in support of allied forces (ARVN, the Army of the Republic of Vietnam) during the Laotian incursion, he was caught in an ambush and died from the explosion of an RPG (rocket propelled grenade).

Because I was within days of my DEROS (Date of Expected Return from Overseas Service) and the end of my two-year enlistment, our unit's commanding officer assigned me to travel back with the body as an official military escort. Within a few days, we flew out of Tan Son Nhut Air Force Base to Hawaii and on to Oakland, California.

Tucked away in my pocket on that journey was a letter addressed to Stephen's family with which he'd entrusted me some months earlier. Composed before he began going into the field, and including several postscripts as those operations continued, it made clear that, should anything happen to him, they were all to understand he had chosen this path. He insisted that he had never felt his life more meaningful than it was in his role as reporter, documenting for the nation the heroism and selflessness of his fellow soldiers.

4

Presenting my own travel papers to military liaisons at Travis Air Force Base in California, I was eventually sent across the bay to the San Francisco Airport and flew east from there on a commercial flight. Through some mix-up, I was not on the same plane as Steve. I was a failed escort.

We reconnected, however, at Dover Air Force Base, and we would ride together in a hearse to Stephen's hometown. Before that short journey, I had to be issued the correct dress uniform, something the Delaware personnel thought should have been done elsewhere along my route. I could offer no narrative about that other than that I had presented my papers to the appropriate officials at each point in my travel. But again I had not performed the duties of an escort very well.

In a room adjacent to the morgue, where I saw a number of mortuary affairs specialists preparing remains for burial, I was outfitted with a uniform that probably was intended for a dead man. They would be the clothes I wore home to Virginia, the ones that hang to this day in the closet of my upstairs bedroom.

An officer and another enlisted man, who had performed escort duties before, were in charge of the process from Dover to Princeton. With one exception, I simply did as I was instructed. Perhaps in violation of military policy—which could, for all I knew, have dictated I surrender Stephen's letter to the Army when I learned of his

5

death—I handed it to Steve's father as soon as I could speak to him alone.

When it was clear I would be in Princeton for several days before the funeral, the Warners insisted I stay with them at their home rather than in quarters provided by the Army. I slept in Stephen's bed. Because I had no civilian clothes, they asked me to wear some of his; and, of course, I complied. I ate at their table. In an unhappy exchange, it seemed as if I was, for forty-eight hours, Steve Warner having come home from war. We all wept, however, on the day he was buried, as the bugle sounded taps, the guns saluted, the flag was folded.

Stephen had such vision in 1971 that, in that same epistle, he instructed his family, should he not return alive, they were to donate his journal, his letters, and his pictures to his undergraduate institution, Gettysburg College. Some of them are available today online at that library's special collections website; and there is now a Center for the Promotion of Peace and Conflict Resolution inspired in part by Stephen's life and writing. In 2003, Gettysburg alumnus Arthur J. Amchan's *Killed In Action: The Life And Times Of Sp4 Stephen H. Warner, Draftee, Journalist And Anti-war Activ*ist was published by Amchan Publishing; it includes a detailed account of his life and writing.

When the Warner family took me to a local motel after the service and a family reception at their house, I could only speculate about what would happen to any of us in the future. For the parents and sister, there would never be a resumption of life before Vietnam. I recognized how fortunate I was.

Inside the motel restaurant, I found my wife having dinner with that generous friend and co-worker, who'd made the special effort to help reunite a married couple. The other friend who'd shared the apartment with my wife was moving in with another student; but she remained close to be a support for us both. In that moment in a New Jersey motel restaurant, then, I reconnected a past with a present civilian life.

Still, I was not yet completely out of the military: I had to report in the morning to Ft. Dix, New Jersey, to be processed out of the service; and my wife had to return to Virginia with her friend to be back at work on Monday morning. I don't recall any particular anger or frustration at the red tape involved in being issued material, filling out forms, receiving my final pay. After all, I was home.

At some point—perhaps that Monday or the next day—I was officially released, DD 214 (Certificate of Release or Discharge from Active Duty) in hand. I retained a commitment to the Army reserves, but knew that, in nearly all cases, that meant four years of inactive duty. I flew from New Jersey to Washington, D.C, and travelled farther to Richmond, only an hour and a half from the little town in which my wife had been teaching school during my absence. There I experienced a final delay.

It was too late at night to ask her to drive down, pick me up, bring me home, and still be ready for her classes the next morning. I was prepared to rent a car at the airport, but, having only cash, I was turned down by every company. They would only take credit cards. Finally, I went to the bus station downtown, where a bus would leave at something like 4:00 in the morning. Again, this was not a painful experience, considering where I'd been.

At something like 6:00 the next morning, I called my wife from the local station, and she drove less than a mile to take me, with all my belongings stuffed into a single duffle bag, and return to our apartment. She left almost immediately, and I slept that day, content that all was well and that all would be well.

It has been.

But there is, among other things, survivor's guilt. I was home safe; others were not. And the meaning of that fundamental fact has over forty years knit its way into my consciousness and become intertwined with my fellow church member's prayer for the fallen men of an earlier war. Doing such things as visit the Vietnam Veterans Memorial in the nation's capital, read accounts of other conflicts, see the nation return to war in the twenty-first century has inspired me to pray for my generation and to compose these stories, which I hope, may be helpful to others.

They are not all sad, though some are. Most involve the assimilation of hard choices and unlucky events into productive lives. And these stories also feature those who accept veterans back into their world after service, often understanding in profound ways what can or must be done for healing to occur. Again, my wife's two friends inspire some of the fictional characters you are about to meet who help in similar ways.

T. S. Eliot said that in our beginning is our end, and in our end is our beginning. So, I start this collection with what I thought was the end of my experience, a sad day in Princeton, New Jersey. But as that same day inaugurated a forty-year effort to understand the months that immediately preceded it, it is also a beginning. I pray for those who continue to take up such struggles and ask you do the same.

~~~

How to Not Tell a War Story

They all knew they were going to die. Not by the occasional rocket, less frequent mortar round, or stray bullets from hot firefights across Cam Ranh Bay, but because of some stupid, fucking accident. Show-Me would be reading a letter from Sandra back home in Fairfield and step in front of a deuce-and-a-half, not going so fast but with such momentum that he felt only a slap on the side of his head. High on a dozen Falstaffs from the E-4 club, Bernard the Jew, having survived the projects in Brooklyn with no father at home, would fail to see the warning tape and fall into a construction hole. He lay in the shape of a crowbar for two days, his neck broken. And John-john, who had not yet grown up, was convinced he suffered from undiagnosed allergies. He was stung by a scorpion and died in his bed, genitals swollen to the size of a bowling pin and . . .well, bowling balls. So they prophesied.

It didn't happen, despite past events that inspired such likelihood. And, naturally, they wanted their own stories to stop short of tragedy.

There had been, after all, Janowsky and Sharp. Well, several tours back, but, still . . . dead, dead, dead they were.

It was Tet one year later, and some mad sapper, recalling what had been perceived around the world as a victory for the North, got through the perimeter and heaved a grenade before the flares went up and he was obliterated by the towers. But Sharp and Janowsky, so they said, came apart in their bunker. It could happen again, or nearly so.

And Smith, plain old Smith, the Smitty. Two weeks from DEROS, he was hand-carrying his papers — the safest way, as they, the United States Army of Clerks, knew — and couldn't believe the siren was for real. They were giving drops, for Christ's sake!

Nixon was determined to demonstrate that the war was winding down and troops were coming home, so tours were being cut short by a week, two weeks, three. Smith, suddenly a short-timer, would be on his Freedom Bird almost a month before he had expected. At the siren's scream, he scanned the sky to prove nothing was there. He must have seen the damn rocket itself as it slammed into the ground in front of him and then detonated. "Don't mean nothin,'" said Bernie.

But Butterball's story was the worst. Volunteering out of boredom to ride the mail run to Nha Trang, he was hit somewhere west of Na Tia, a lone rifleman firing blindly at the roar of a chopper above him. Butterball had passed Day 183 and could see nothing to hope for, now that his week in Bangkok was over. "What the hell, see some of the country," he shrugged, pulling on a beer the night before. "What the country, see some of hell," they parodied in the bar who-knows-who had built at one end of the hootch. Butterball didn't see much.

What pissed them off, of course, was that, in the end, they had no war stories to tell. "Is that all there is," they heard; "is that all there is?"

At first, back in the World, they didn't want to talk. They were mostly draftees or men who enlisted to get (they were promised) better assignments (either they didn't get them or didn't keep them for long). So they had never anticipated their veteran status. In-country, they didn't know what to look for that, recounted later, would inspire awe. And, then, after it was over, they had no audience. This war was so unlike others, they came to believe, that it couldn't offer heroes; and mere service was nothing.

Most of the REMFs had at least some college; a few were graduates. When Congress went to a lottery system instead of the draft, local boards met their quotas with the more educated, older men added to their depleted pools. For many getting drafted was a failure of education, of social standing, of sophistication.

"There's a college in my hometown," an almost embarrassed Blessing explained. "A lot of professors' kids are in school or graduate school. When they stopped deferments, they came after my ass."

"A lot of my buddies got in the Reserves or the National Guard," lamented John-john. "But I didn't have the connections. I signed up to play clarinet in a marching band, but here I fucking am." It had taken him longer than most to get used to using "fuck" in every other sentence. Now that he had the hang of it, he seemed to believe it granted him instant maturity.

Bernie could not quite squelch a sense of duty to preserve the country that had rescued his mother, if not the rest of his family, from the Holocaust. He thought Vietnam a terrible lie, but he wouldn't take the medical deferment his mother hinted he could get from "a friend of a friend, Doctor Dontkilloursons."

Of course, lifers were not so pleased to have soldiers who proved more difficult to manage than fresh high school graduates or dropouts. True, basic training quotas took the majority for 11-Bravos and other combat MOSs, but the less unlucky former college students joined a far-reaching network of clerks who figured out the system and often used this knowledge for their own ends rather than to complete the mission. Even in Vietnam, paper pushers wielded power. However, their ability to misfile folders, to ask for more signatures, to inspire a review of procedure later made at best cocktail chatter, not war stories.

So, back home and in the career paths from which they'd taken temporary leave, they knit together pasts that jumped over their military years. Mostly, they were pleased few asked what it had been like. The glimpses they'd had of the real thing could not be assimilated into civilian conversation with their old friends or new acquaintances. Woken from troubling dreams, they told their wives, girlfriends, family that any

13

screams or cries or whimpers were unrelated to their Southeast Asia experience, a mystery to themselves as well. Vaguely, though, they wished there were connections, war stories they could tell.

Blessing did have his anecdotes to amuse colleagues in Human Resources, black humor emphasizing his mastery of irony and liberal politics. "The best dodge I knew about was Chesterfield, a fraternity brother. He had survived basic, was in his third week of AIT, well aware than in a few months his ass would in be in the 'Nam. Straining to take a crap in one of those open stalls with half the platoon waiting their turns, he herniated himself."

The former Show-me always looked for places to use key phrases—"bust a gut," "crap out," "no stomach for it"—but seldom found the right opportunity.

"They could repair it, of course?" he would be asked.

"Well, yes, but, we pointed out to him, if he declined treatment by the Army, he could get a medical discharge. He'd have to pay civilian doctors for the surgery, but . . . but that's just money."

"So that's what he did?"

Blessing opened his eyes wider and looked directly at them. They would pause, then nod in understanding—ah, yes, of course, we all would.

14

He also liked his in-country training story. All newbies had go to go through several days of orientation soon after they arrived. Blessing had the runs so bad when he was supposed to report that he ended up in sickbay instead. Several weeks after he got out, he found a certificate of completion on his desk, a gift from his fellow clerks. He could still, he would later tell his stateside audience, escape captors by camouflaging himself as a banana tree, survive in the jungle by trapping monkeys for food, travel by the stars until he reached friendly forces and/or USO Donut Dollies.

He never told them, though, that when he went on guard duty the first time, he didn't know how to assemble the grenade launcher, or keep from burning his hands on an M60 barrel, or work the field radio. And he blotted from his own memory how frightened he'd been when his buddy in the bunker, Giordano, said to wake him if he was needed, then fell asleep so hard Blessing was sure he was dead. Tony's had his throat cut in the dark by a VC machete, Blessing thought, his bowels loosening.

As the years passed, he stopped telling even these stories, believing that the Vietnam War had melded into history, become fixed in a narrative of corrupt and stupid politicians, anti-war protests, angry soldiers who came home feeling betrayed or crazed by guilt. The nation had moved on, so he and his buddies had to as well.

Then came 9/11, Afghanistan, and the Iraq wars. A new national attitude toward soldiers emerged. "Blame the war, not the warrior," the people said and held parades for returning troops. Service became noble again, and the patriotism of WWII seemed almost to have been resurrected. Blessing went downtown and applauded when a local National Guard unit marched past on the way to reunion with their families. Where were the Welcomes Home for the Vietnam U.S. Army of Clerks?

"We were spit on," John-john, now a successful, middle-aged real estate agent, wrote from Minneapolis. "They called us baby killers."

Of course, that was something he saw on television, not a personal experience. But Show-me agreed. "I can count on one hand the number of people who have thanked me for my service. And that's over thirty years' time!"

"They get all the PTSD they want while we've got Agent Orange running out our butts."

Of course, Cam Ranh Bay was hardly a toxic site. John-john had suffered more from sunburn at the base's fine beach.

Recalling the fatalistic mantra of that time, Bernie wrote, "There it is."

Back in Brooklyn, he'd done better than the rest to integrate his Army years with the whole of his life. A New York City public relations officer, he joined the Vietnam Veterans of America and worked with support groups for military families.

Still, when the courage of NFL star Tillman was referred to, or Jessica Lynch was rescued, they all found themselves thinking back to their long-ago tours. Did they have stories?

Giordano had gone into the burning mess hall, convinced that Blair was still in there. But that seemed more a civilian act than the battlefield valor they were trying to configure.

Had they missed something else? Maybe memory had played tricks on them, obscuring what would now come to light at last. Back then, they hadn't studied forms for the narration of danger, but now, more aware, could they reshape their experience for the new era?

The details had originally fit into a standard model. When the chopper came down at 9th Field Hospital, they couldn't find an entry wound. But the man's shoulders and the back of his fatigues were soaked with blood. Finding the damage to his spine and skull, they stabilized him for immediate transport to Japan.

Word came back two weeks later that provided an explanation, whether true or not. The round had entered his anus so perfectly that no marks were noticeable. Medical personnel assumed the blood they saw there had drained from the body cavity. Butterball's memory of the event had been erased, and his mental capacity after the injury was restricted, so he could offer no account himself of what happened.

At the time, his buddies couldn't help turning it into the worst kind of story. "The VC cut him a new one," lamented Bernie.

"Screwed up the ass by Vietnam," crowed a less sympathetic hootch-mate, "just like the rest of us." John-john, asserting his status, announced "The New and Improved Rear Fucked Mother Echelon."

Blessing heard Peggy Lee sing "And a beautiful lady in pink tights flew high above our heads" and wondered if she had been entered.

Somehow they felt justified in making their jokes. Butterball had boasted that it was what he did, when the price wasn't too high, to the whores they visited at the bar outside the gate. The others felt you shouldn't give details, let alone brag. And it was sick, anyway, something a fat Californian like him would think of. Was what happened to him some kind of cosmic justice?

Blessing found that he couldn't tell the story in any other way, especially not now, not when genuine commitment deserved expression. However, learning that Tillman had probably been the victim of friendly fire, and that Jessica Lynch wouldn't confirm the official narrative, they began to wonder if Vietnam really was so different from other wars. In degree perhaps, but not in kind.

They'd all been thankful to have safe duty, what they thought of as the luck of the draw. This was the price: one REMF's misfortune didn't measure up to battlefield loss. It was more like a car accident, cancer, the act of God.

Then the Walter Reed fiasco came to light. Blessing saw it on television and was stunned. The faces of the families got to him: lost, pained, despairing. After all the public support for what the military had been called to do, the country found them in decaying quarters, in paperwork labyrinths, at treatment limbo.

His wife retold the experience of a college student in their church. Varsity soccer player, she and her team had been taken to visit patients at the Kansas City Veterans Affairs Medical Center. But there they saw only the less serious cases, those who could testify to good treatment, a functioning bureaucracy. When the story broke, the student was furious.

Some of Blessings' colleagues brushed it off as what was to be expected. They insisted that these wounded warriors had known what they were in for when they joined the "all-volunteer" military. Blessing felt that term had a vaguely distasteful aura about it, as if soldiers had asked for traumatic brain injury or amputated limbs. He knew from his own experience that many enlisted troops were looking for career training, a way to pay for college, escape from failed social systems. The patients and spouses and parents he saw had been hollowed out, used and discarded.

19

And he knew the crime wasn't just that we put them "in harm's way," as politicians piously acknowledged. We paid them to do what we didn't want to do ourselves, what was so horrific and dehumanizing that the latest generation could not accept it unless translated into digitally constructed video. With the brilliance of animation, the nation had substituted a bloodless slaughter and dazzling recovery for flag-draped coffins rolling down the tarmac of Dover Air Force Base. He wouldn't watch any of the new war movies.

Blessing had once gone to see Butterball, whose real name was Christopher Shepherd.

Sandra couldn't understand why he went.

"It's been fifteen years. Why do you want to go now?"

"I'm not sure I can say. But I got a good flight to L.A. I'll be back the day after tomorrow, the weekend."

The surprise was how happy Chris, who had the mind of a ten-year-old, was. He couldn't move his legs, could barely operate his mechanized wheelchair, had to be fed, diapered, medicated.

"I love Saturday mornings," he told Blessing. "The cartoons, you know. Scooby Doo and . . . and Smurfs. . . and . . ." He was gesturing with one finger.

His mother helped him. "And the Muppets—Fonzi and Kermit. Big Bird."

"Yeah, yeah. I like Grover. He's my . . . he's my hero."

If this weren't hard enough, Show-me couldn't believe Butterball's family. The Shepherds were so grateful he had survived, that he was back with them.

"We count our blessings every day. I'm sure your parents do, too. Are you married?"

"Yes. We have . . . we have two children, a boy and a girl."

"Will you pray with us? We have so much to be thankful for."

He actually got down on his knees with them, astounded that they were not devastated by what had happened. In his own head, he heard a variation of what Peggy Lee asked: "Why don't they just end it all?" and her response: "When that final moment comes and I'm breathing my last breath, I'll be saying to myself, is that all there is, is that all there is?"

It wasn't all there is, but it took more years before he began to find words for it.

He saw *The News Hour* on PBS. Tim O'Brien was being interviewed two decades after the appearance of his quintessential book on Vietnam, *The Things They Carried*. Blessing bought the book the next day, hoping to find out what he carried.

One chapter narrated the death of a grunt who steps on a bobby trap and is blown up into a tree — well, blown all over the tree. The event is told in stages, obliquely, contextualized among other events and later associations. Despite careful repetitions and revisions, it's not clear whether the truth is fully realized.

Blessing wouldn't say he understood the story, but he felt that it represented something profound. The voice of a survivor, however hurt. The refusal to bury the horror even when you want to do so. The insistence on making others look.

Their war had not been different from other wars, he concluded sadly. It was ugly, meaningless, inhuman. But there had been faith. Some had cared, but it was tragic, foolish, insane. It was pointless, revolting, ungodly. But many endured.

He called Bernie. "Remember Butterball?"

"Stupid fucking accident," he responded. They talked for an hour.

The Ugly Sweater Holiday Party

I.

A white, 65-year-old, Midwestern male of Scandinavian descent, he hadn't dressed up for Halloween after the age of seven. There were no tattoos or piercings on his body. His fashion goal, in fact, was to go unnoticed. How could he attend an "Ugly Sweater Holiday Party" (or, as the invitation explained in a footnote, "Ugly Holiday Sweater Party")?

If he went, Bruce decided, it would be wearing what he always did for such social occasions—khakis, a dress shirt with no tie, sport jacket. But he knew he would have to resist being pressured by Samantha to find some kind of sweater. "Hemmed in," he punned to himself.

The party would be a week before Christmas, and the guests—most of them academics like himself—would make the usual reports on family travel, the snide comments about commercialization of the season (though few took the holidays as anything more than vacation days), observations about the weather compared to "the winter of whenever."

Hmm. Wait a minute. Could he find that old thing?

It was in a trunk outside the guest bedroom—in surprisingly good shape. Of course, it had only been worn that once. He found exactly the unattractive orange he remembered, an undistinguished pattern, commonplace wool. And it brought back irritating memories—perfect for the event.

It would be a tight fit, of course, after all those years in which his middle-age spread had developed; but he could stand it for one evening. At the end of the night, however, the ugly sweater provided not so much an escape from the ordinary as an escape into the ordinary—for himself and Samantha, at least.

Bruce had bought the sweater on R&R forty years earlier. Well, on his way to R&R.

Packing the only clothes he had (all warm-weather), he flew out of Cam Rahn Bay, South Vietnam, in December 1970, crammed into a charter jet with several hundred other GIs headed for Hawaii. Samantha was to meet him there, having taken a week's leave from teaching elementary school and traveling out of St. Louis to Honolulu. She had winter clothes (it was December) and summer clothes (she always thought ahead). They would celebrate their second wedding anniversary and their third Christmas together during his seven-day leave.

Bruce hadn't known he would have that three-hour layover in Okinawa. Who paid attention to such details when all you wanted to do is leave Vietnam behind you for a week? He was happy to go anywhere away from that tedium interrupted by terror, but how much more exciting to anticipate a week-long vacation in paradise? Of course, it wasn't all he had hoped. Well, it was and it wasn't. First there were setbacks.

II.

To begin with, the nearly deserted airport in Okinawa was (to him) freezing. With all those other lonely (and horny) men already tired of each other, he was pacing the narrow concourse looking for ways to pass the time. He couldn't concentrate on the book he carried (ironically, *Catch-22*, the WW II story of a man caught between impossible alternatives). And the chilly temperature made it hard to sit still (they must have been saving money by shutting things up during the night).

It had never occurred to Bruce that he might need warmer clothes than those he'd been wearing for the last seven months. That week setting up the new relay station down in the Mekong Delta had been worse than being in an oven wrapped with towels pre-soaked in sweat. And the rest of his time could only be described as baked rather than broiled. But before long in Okinawa he was ready to hug himself in newspapers of any language, if that was all he could find.

Then, at whatever later hour of the night or early hour in the morning it was, a single middle-aged woman opened a small concession stand.

Lifting the wooden front panel, she revealed candy bars, magazines, and newspapers packed on narrow shelves . . . as well as a single rack of clothes!

Bruce wondered if he could meet Samantha in the form-fitting cowboy shirt for sale there (had the Lone Ranger passed through and left this behind?). How about a slim, hideous grey Nehru jacket (garb of an Asian diplomat or the Beatles at Shea Stadium, 1965)? Wait, here's a sweater!

He bought it without calculating the expense or testing the size. It shrank the small amount of money he'd been saving for all the things they wanted to do: see the island outside of Honolulu, swim in the ocean, go to a luau. But he wanted to be warm. This got him through the first setback.

III.

"What is wrong with this bed!" he exclaimed the next night. They were staying at The Stupa, one of the luxury hotels recommended to Army family members. Resembling a pagoda in structure, it was famous for the koi pond that surrounded its famous floating restaurant. Giant gold carp swam freely among the lilies, and orchids of all colors and sizes decorated the walkways.

Frustrated, Bruce jumped up and studied the bed. It seemed a perfectly normal length, not some version that, he was speculating, had been shortened for the smaller Orientals peopling this island. Six feet tall himself, he couldn't straighten his legs out all the way.

The rest of the furniture looked standard, of higher quality than the places they'd stayed when traveling the states and full-sized, comfortable-looking. Sam had made all the arrangements from Missouri, not telling him that her parents had insisted on expanding her budget.

"It's fine," she told him, lifting the sheet to show her specially bought negligee. "Get back in here with me."

They'd already made love once earlier in the day, but in a kind of frenzy on top of the bed. He was pleased that she had been eager then and seemed to be again. At least those deliberately repressed fears had been eased.

"Why can't I stretch out in there? Something's not right." He padded the foot of the bed, as if he suspected it had a hidden compartment stuffed with papaya, guava, and pineapple where his feet should go. Some damned magician's trick box.

Sam sat up and looked at her feet, which pushed up the sheet and a light blanket right where they should. "You're imagining things. You could just be . . . tight. You know, adjusting to the fact that you're not . . . back there."

He realized this was an important moment: he had to keep himself under control. An explosion here could spoil the whole week.

While they'd only been married two years, at twenty-five, he was older than most of the men in his unit. And he understood before he left Vietnam that he and Sam would be nervous. Keep the lid on, he'd told himself over and over.

"You're right. I . . . I must be imagining it." He pulled back the covers on his side and slipped into the bed again, putting his arm across her waist and rising on his elbow to kiss her. She lifted her head, and her hair, which she'd let grow out while he was away, fell back from her face. My God, she was beautiful!

He pulled back again. "Ah, come on!" he said, but more in bemusement than anger. "Look." He was pushing his feet against something at the end of the bed. They stopped where hers did.

This time she got out and pulled off the covers. Standing with her hands on her hips at the side of the bed, she exclaimed, "Why in the world would anyone do this?"

The bed had been short-sheeted, the top sheet folded under itself at the bottom of the bed rather than being inserted between the end of the mattress and the box springs. The bottom edge was pulled back under itself about a foot-and-a-half, then the edges were tucked in tightly on both sides. Sam's feet didn't reach the crease, but Bruce's slipped over the tucked-in portion and ran into the fold.

Bruce surveyed the bed and then tugged the top sheet. "Wait a minute. This isn't a queen-sized

28

bed sheet; it's a double sheet put crossways on the bed."

"You're right! It's not wide enough for this bed. They must not have enough queen bed sheets for some reason — maybe the laundry broke down — so they hoped we were short people."

"Or they were five sheets to the wind!"

They called room service, got new sheets, went back to bed chuckling. They had survived a second crisis.

IV.

The accident was worse.

After a delightful, sightseeing drive into the mountains and a picnic swim at Waikiki Beach, Bruce had forgotten being forced to buy a sweater he didn't want and the foot-scrunching hotel bed. He and Sam were only a few blocks from the Stupa, where they'd made reservations to eat at the floating restaurant, when a woman, who spoke no English, and was driving a rusted out Chevrolet Corvair, hit them from behind.

No one was hurt, though Bruce's seat belt stuck and he was pinned in the driver's seat for an uncomfortable several minutes. He'd cut off the ignition immediately, but didn't — in the event of a fire — want to be trapped. He also feared secondary collisions, and his door was jammed.

"You okay, sir?" asked a man at his window. Bruce was still struggling to get unhooked.

"I will be in just a minute. I need to get this damn belt loose." He was tugging it every direction he could. Traffic had stopped, at least, and the danger seemed over. Sam was fine.

The man opened the driver's side door and flashed a policeman's badge. "Let me see if I can help." Bruce was relieved—and amazed that a law enforcement officer was on the scene so quickly. But the rescuer had no more luck with the seat belt than Bruce had.

Sam, studying the situation from her side of the car, told them both to stop yanking on things. Putting a hand on Bruce's arm, she said, "Suck in your tummy, sweetie."

"What?"

"Make yourself tiny, big man."

When he did, pressing his rear end into the car seat as hard as he could, the pressure came off the buckle, and she was able to push the release button. "You're free! No hold on your record. Ha-ha!" And they thought that ended the affair.

Well, the officer did take down names, car rental information, driver's license numbers. He explained that he had actually been in the car behind the lady who hit the Nilssons. His brakes didn't hold for some reason, and he bumped her into them—chain reaction, but not serious. There seemed to be no damage to the rental car, though

30

some minor dents and scrapes were found on the back of woman's compact vehicle.

"You don't have to worry," the friendly officer told them. "I'll file all the forms. I was off-duty, but I can take care of it for you. You're on R & R, aren't you?"

"Right. I'd be happy not to have to spend a lot of time on this." He had imagined himself waiting hours at a police station, squeezed on a bench between an odiferous homeless man and a frightfully overweight prostitute.

"You deserve that, my friend. Go on back to the hotel . . . ." He glanced across the seat, inspecting Samantha, and smiled. "Enjoy . . . the island."

Bruce was proud that the man appreciated Sam's beauty. She'd worn her hair short all her life, but decided to let it grow — a surprise — while he was overseas. She had been attractive with it neat and close, but the shoulder length cut made her almost glamorous. He knew he wanted her above him in bed, his face framed in a tent of her dark curls.

The phone call the next morning was completely unexpected.

Putting his palm firmly over the receiver, Bruce mouthed to Sam. "The police!"

It was almost 9:00, but they were still in bed. She raised her eyebrows.

"Now?" Bruce asked. "Here?"

Apparently there had been problems reporting the accident, and the Chief of Internal Affairs wanted to talk with them. Bruce tried to explain how he and his wife were on their fourth day of R & R and that their time to learn about local culture was being cut short. He asked if this couldn't be done on the phone, but the Chief was politely insistent. He said he would come to their room in half an hour.

Sam protested by refusing to get up and get dressed. She slipped a robe on over her shoulders but remained in bed, resting back against a stack of pillows, a copy of *Puppet on a Chain* folded over on her lap.

"I'm terribly sorry," Chief Wall began. "It seems there were some irregularities — nothing you did, I'm sure. But I need to verify the facts of this case."

Bruce had no bathrobe, so he'd put on pants and a shirt, refusing to button it all the way or tuck it in. And he was barefoot. "The officer who was on the scene got all the information. What's the problem?"

"Well, that's the problem. He was off duty and not authorized to make the report. He has to call the police like anyone else."

"Will we have to . . . 'go downtown?'" asked Samantha, smiling coyly but not in a combative way.

"No, Ma'am. Not at all. If you can just confirm what I've pieced together from Officer Kalani and Mrs. Pukuit, I'll be . . . out of your way in a matter of minutes."

They did. And gradually they began to appreciate the Chief's kindness in coming to them. In almost any other circumstance, they would have been called down to the station, required to fill out forms, made to confirm their identities, insurance policies, reasons for travel. The third crisis was over.

V.

The Christmas luau exceeded their expectations.

They had trouble at first shopping for family and friends in a summer climate. The store's Menehune Santa had the traditional red hat and white beard, but wore a bright aloha shirt and beach shorts. Norfolk Island pine and palm trees replaced the expected cedars or firs, while outdoor displays often featured an outrigger canoe drawn by dolphins instead of a sleigh behind reindeer.

Still, Sam insisted, it was a once-in-a-lifetime opportunity; so they learned to say "Mele Kalikimaka," to hum along with traditional carols in different languages accompanied by guitar, to eat sweet potato cheesecake with "haupia," or coconut, frosting. Eventually macadamia nut clusters, toy ukuleles, hula girl spice sets, and coconut postcards were being shipped, or would be carried back, in time for the holiday. Bruce, who would have chafed at hours spent in the mall back home, was relaxed carrying her packages and approving her choices "I'm not in the 'Nam," Bruce reminded himself more than once.

But the Beachcomber luau was the best. It was in an open courtyard on the hotel grounds, twilight in the permanently glorious weather highlighted by flaming torches. After he and Sam had attempted the hula 'auana, feasted on both kalua pig and lomi salmon, savored a pineapple sparkling wine, satisfaction set in so fully that it blocked out the fact that they had only one more night in paradise.

At the end of the show fabled entertainer Don Ho performed his signature, "Tiny Bubbles." Bruce hadn't ever felt he could sing himself, but was swept away when Sam threw her arms around his neck and, looking into his eyes, began to croon the responses to Ho's verse: "Tiny Bubbles" "(tiny bubbles)"; "in the wine" "(in the wine)".

A thousand flowers whose names he couldn't know scented the breeze. Bruce felt they were breaking free of gravity, their souls rising together into the tropical night, the sky opening for them.

"Here's to the golden moon," crooned Sam. "Here's to the silver sea." And he sang back:

34

"Here's a kiss that will not fade away." She put her head on his shoulder, her lips to his ear: "I'm gonna love you till the end of time."

Even as his plane raced down the Honolulu tarmac the next day to take him back to hell, he felt elated. All the irritating little things they'd encountered—the short-sheeted bed, being locked in the car seat, squeezed by a policeman's self-serving—were, he realized, the problems of everyday life in The World, foretaste of what he longed to confront for the rest of his life.

What a fool he had been to complain to Sam, when, unlike Underwood, he was alive and well.

VI.

Forty years later, pulling the sweater over his head, he recalled tiny bubbles of Hawaiian happiness in the winter of his discontent. The orange wool chafed his neck, and he felt the sweater bind at the waist. But he took a deep breath, and his lungs filled easily, as if they were drawing in the spirit of that earlier occasion, not just the air of today.

"I know that sweater!" Sam said, coming upstairs to see what was keeping him. She already had on her Santa-plus-elves-plus-reindeer-plus sleigh-plus-toys-plus-chimneys sweater. "Wherever did you find it?"

"You remember it?"

"I could never forget."

He wrapped her in his arms and kissed her. "You kept me warm then. Let me keep you warm now."

VII.

At the Ugly Sweater Holiday Party (or Ugly Holiday Sweater Party), the hostess looked him over and said, "Let me guess. You bought this at Famous-Barr on Black Friday in . . . um, 1970. A bargain you couldn't resist, right?"

Bruce paused for just a moment. "Exactly!" he said, looking at Samantha. "How ever did you know?"

~~~

Writing in the Sand

Writing in the sand was a euphemism for taking a leak.

Outside the Cam Rhan Bay enlisted men's club, they relieved themselves at the latrine—a bunch of pipes stuck in the ground over a soakage pit. As the night went on, they didn't always hit a pipe. It was a happy illusion that they were scripting philosophical insights on the ground when, in fact, their language was disintegrating into drivel . . . or dribble.

Most nights in February and March of 1970, the gang of 73D (accounting specialist Madison), 81B (technical drafting specialist Jackson), 71Qs/Rs (print/radio journalists Adams/Penn), and 75B (personnel administration specialist Jefferson) gathered at the end of their shifts to buy each other rounds until they could no longer walk, talk, or piss straight.

There was something about standing out under the stars, mountains behind them, the South China Sea in front of them, that led to pontification—especially after half a dozen beers. When one of the group returned to the table, it was likely he would make a pronouncement. Only one, though, shaped the future for them.

Penn established the custom. Coming back from a solo excursion, he interrupted Madison, who'd been saying how much he'd like to dance with the Philippine band's mini-skirted singer.

("Dance" was another euphemism.) She'd been rotating her hips in a smooth, easy motion as she caressed, with her unclassifiable accent, the lyrics of the Carpenters' "Close to You."

"Every time I take a leak," Penn said, "I look up at the stars and feel some sort of revelation coming on."

"Madison's got a something else on," said Jefferson and hit his neighbor on the shoulder.

Penn dismissed them both. "I'm serious. This is what I've realized: when I get home, I'm going to make a million dollars."

"Yeah, aren't we all."

"Listen up! I'm a country-and-western songwriting machine. And a minute ago, out there—" he waved his hand through the corrugated metal wall, "—out there I got the words for another big hit." He was an information specialist, drafted a month after he had started at Boss Radio, KHJ, in Los Angeles.

"Okay," said Jefferson. "Lay it on us." They all hoisted their beers in anticipation of toasting genius.

Penn grinned, raised a finger in one hand and his Falstaff in the other. "Here's the title: 'Wishing on a star in Vietnam, while Jody gives my honey the wham-bam-bam.'" Jody was the mythical boy back home who made time with the GI's girl when he was overseas. "It starts this way: 'When honey wore her short shorts back at home, Old Jody walked behind her and wanted some.'"

"Enough! Stop! We'll buy it." Penn's buddies groaned, but found his composition a perfectly adequate reason to drink. And, as they came to realize in the coming weeks, this moment had opened a channel for the expression of repressed desires, secret fears, and desperate aspiration. They also hoped it would help them forget Danny Tract—or, as they grimly called him, Sub Tract.

Adams (71Q) offered the phrase, "writing in the sand," as a name for the ritual. It was an allusion to the old Ozark folk tale, "Pissing in the Snow." His father's uncle had told it to him, irreverently, at the reception after his grandmother's funeral, and Carl repeated it to his buddies to christen the new practice.

"There was these two neighbors down by Tuscumbia, farms side by side along the Osage. The children had gone to school and worked in the fields together, but one day the first farmer said to the other, 'That boy of yours oughtn't be coming 'round here no more.'"

Adams was doing his version of hillbilly speak. Penn raised his eyebrows.

"He looked pretty angry," Adams continued, "so the second farmer asked, 'Why, what's he done now? Sure, he gits into his share of trouble, but he ain't that bad.'"

"His friend scowled, 'Well, t'other night, he pissed in the snow right by our porch!'"

"Maybe he oughtn't done that," admitted the other. "But, hell, you and me done worse when we was his age. He's just growin' up, is all.'"

"The first farmer was still agitated. 'Dammit, he wrote Sadie's name, spelled it out clear as can be where anyone could read it.'"

Jefferson chuckled as if he saw the punch line coming, but he hadn't a clue.

"The second farmer couldn't help chucklin'," Adams explained. "'I'll tell him not to be doing that. But, shoot, that's still ain't so terrible you should take offense.'"

"'Don't you see?' his friend went on. 'There was two sets of tracks in the snow, and, by damn, I know my own daughter's handwriting when I see it!'"

That brought the guffaws . . . and another round. Adams was surprised at how homesick recounting that tale made him, his Missouri past somehow more precious than he'd ever thought it could be.

All the revelations did not come in one night, of course, but over six weeks' time it seemed each man had a least one epiphany, and some had more. Jackson, a physics major at Princeton before he was drafted, now an 81B, asserted a cosmological truth.

"Boys," he said, scanning the faces of his audience. "Looking at Orion up there tonight, I recalled that the earth is round, but the universe is only curved."

Most had no idea what he was saying.

He continued. "Einstein proved, as you know, that space is curved." This produced, nods, head shakes, rolling eyes. 'Sooo . . . ," Jackson concluded, "if we cut straight across the universe, we travel in time."

"Ah," said Adams. "So you took a whiz in south Jersey tonight, zipped up a week from tomorrow in New Mexico, and zipped around to Cam Rahn Bay to drink with us."

"Exactly! But here's the good news, my friend: you have no need to keep that short-timer calendar." The number of days left in-country — plus a wake-up — was known to every soldier, and it was usually inscribed on a pin-up calendar featuring Chris Noel or Joy Wilkerson. Jackson concluded, "You're not short, you see. Across the curve of space-time, you're already home."

"To home," proposed Penn, and cans went up and beer down.

The momentary elation at the reduction of their numbers to DEROS, of course, didn't last. This time Jefferson had his eyes on the band's singer. "I think I'll stay here a bit longer," he decided.

"Keep your pants on, lover boy."

Jefferson's writing in the sand was easier to understand in the end: you remake yourself through DOD forms.

"Here it is," the 75B declared. "I saw it in the cloud graffiti, which said—and I shit you not—it said 'Use the STP 10-92M15-SM-TG.'"

"Oh, yeah," agreed Jackson. "That will transfer you to Sweden where you can get a sex change operation and have a movie made about you: 'What Happened to my Whatever they Were.'"

"No, asshole, I become a mortuary affairs specialist."

"An undertaker?"

"Right."

"There must be a punch line here somewhere."

"Well, you know there are no real undertakers over here. They bag the bodies, freeze them, fly them to The World for burial. So, as soon as I run the papers and show I have a different MOS, they ship me home and assign me to Dover."

"Home to pickle bodies and put them in the ground. A great life!"

"Let me ask you something, Adams." Jefferson had his wizard look on. "Do we ever run out of death?"

Adams had to agree. "Not around here. The grim reaper did get Sub Tract."

The allusion to what they hoped to forget sobered the group as usual. Fortunately, the band broke into a miserable rendition of Credence Clearwater's "I Heard it through the Grapevine," and they chimed in, in an effort to drown out the male vocalist.

It was Madison (73D) who did the numbers. "We're all zeros right now, my friends. But I know how to be Number 1."

"This is not your zero-sum game, is it?" asked Adams. None of them understood his economic models.

"Not a bit of it: I'm talking about the hemline index."

"Okay, we'll bite: what's the hemline index."

"Well, it's been shown that, the higher women's hemlines go, the more the stock market rises."

"Ah, so it's like reading your palm to tell the future, though this time we're reading the . . . the, um, upper, inner, higher, closer length of her thigh?"

"He means her snatch."

"Must every conversation around here descend to the lowest common denominator — the gutter! Listen, economists watch fashion as an indicator of business growth, but, it occurred to me — out under the stars — . . . ."

"It occurred to you," Jefferson interrupted, "out under the stars that your indicator was rising?"

"If there was a skirt going up in the vicinity," added Jackson, "I doubt if we can specify a financial cause."

"At ease!" commanded Madison. "Out under the stars it occurred to me that they've got it all backwards. You don't see if hemlines are changing to guide your investments. You work it the other way around: lower hemlines to buy; raise them to sell."

"And exactly how do you accomplish that?"

"That's the genius part, thank you very much. Since women do everything we men do backwards—in order to drive us crazy and because they're made that way—we start wearing our pants higher to bring skirts—and prices—down. Then reverse to longer pants, sell stock, retire to the Virgin Islands where there are no income taxes."

"To virgins!"

They drank with gusto, not so much because Madison's epiphany was an inspiration but because the reference to pants made them think again of Tract. Adams wondered if they could ever blot those images from their minds.

Jefferson, who'd been Tract's best friend, tried hardest to put it behind him. "'Oh, come with old Khayyam, and leave the Wise to talk," he recited one night, after no one's writing in the sand seemed to answer their need. 'One thing is certain, that Life flies; one thing is certain, and the Rest is Lies; the Flower that once has blown for ever dies.'"

"Blown?" asked Jackson.

"It means 'blossomed,' asshole, like a flower," answered Jefferson. "It's poetry, man. I'm elevating the tone of our conversation."

"To conversation!"

Encouraged, Jefferson recited: "'. . . the Seed of Wisdom did I sow, and with my own hand labour'd it to grow: and this was all the Harvest that I reap'd— I came like Water, and like Wind I go.'"

"You mean our writing in the sand is going to be blown to dust?"

"It sure as hell isn't carved in stone. We've been fooling ourselves, boys. Tract's dead and we might be, too. 'The Moving Finger writes; and, having writ, moves on: nor all thy Piety nor Wit shall lure it back to cancel half a Line . . .'"

Adams looked at the band, deep in an earnest imitation of The Rolling Stones belting out "(I can't get no) Satisfaction!" He turned back to Jefferson. "You're making it damn hard to enjoy a good drunk."

And, after a while, they found they couldn't change the story or create a better one to erase it from their memories.

Danny Tract had been just like the rest of them, a draftee who got lucky and was given a clerical MOS: 75B, personnel administration specialist. He's served a year at Ft. Bragg, North Carolina, interviewing new recruits in basic training and relating their skills and experience to military occupational specialties (even though 95% would be designated 11-Bravo by the Pentagon's computers, no matter what his recommendation). Danny was the last in his unit to get orders for Vietnam, but those who'd gone before and landed in key administrative offices steered his papers to the base personnel office.

Ten months into his tour he went missing. He was the solitary guard on duty from midnight to eight at the Officers' Mess. When he didn't respond on the field phone, they sent a battle-tested sergeant to check on him. Not a sign, vanished, disappeared into thin air.

Well, not completely. They found a letter he must have been writing. Addressed to his girlfriend back in Illinois, it was a mournful confession of loneliness and despair. "Not sure I can make it," he wrote. "I haven't heard from you in six weeks. I need to know you'll be there when I come home. Honey, write to me."

The note was neatly folded, tucked inside an unsealed, addressed envelope, stuck in the crack between the mess door and the frame.

Tract's body washed up a week later on the beach, bloated and obscene. He had drowned, but there was a knot on the back of his head. He might, they said, have fallen, been struck, or collided with some object. There were also odd marks on his wrists and ankles not unlike rope burns. Had he been abducted and killed? Or had he taken his own life by walking into the waves with weights tied to his limbs?

The oddest thing—at least according to the rumors that ran wild around the unit—was that he was fully clothed except for pants. Other stories circulated about mutilation. And since they'd all heard what the VC did to prisoners, they imagined the worst.

After the hemline story Penn declared an end to writing in the sand. However, his *tabula rasa* declaration followed once again a trip to the latrine.

"We have to give up drinking," he insisted, retaking his seat at the table. "A voice spoke to me out of the sky. 'Give up drinking,' it said."

"There must have been a chaplain pi—. . . ah, preaching at the next hole. Did some commandments chiseled on a big rock descend in a cloud?"

Penn appeared to be serious. "It might just have been the voice of God. Look, every night we waste five or six hours here, throwing back beer and talking shit. What the hell do we accomplish? That's time we could be using for something productive. We're going back to the World one of these days, and we need to take advantage of any opportunity we've got to better ourselves."

"To ourselves!" offered Jackson.

"To better ourselves!" proposed Madison, believing he'd already achieved improvement, at least in toasting.

Adams, though, was curious. "How do we better ourselves?"

Penn sighed. "I'm not so sure about that, but maybe take a correspondence course. Or start a chess club. How about learn another language?"

"Oh, yeah, gook talk. Great idea. Then you can extend for a couple more tours, marry a slant-eye, and vote in the next election over here."

Penn set his half empty beer on the table and rose. "You guys do what you want, but I'm tired of falling asleep in my clothes and waking up half pissed. My tongue feels like someone used it for a blotter, and nothing will go in my stomach except coffee until noon."

Adams began to think there was something to this. He rose too. "You know, it all started with Sub Tract. Instead of having just a few beers, after that it's as if we're afraid to stop until we're completely wasted. But it doesn't change what happened. He's under ground in Tennessee, and we're still right here in 'Nam. I'm ready to try something else."

He recalled his tee-totaling grandmother from Steelville, Missouri, who'd been arrested twice at temperance rallies. His Baptist parents didn't disapprove of alcohol, but he'd never seen either of them have more than a glass of champagne at weddings. In college he seldom participated himself in the traditional, booze inspired bull sessions. What was happening to him now?

"I'm calling it Clean Slate," Penn announced. "We start over, as of this moment, with no baggage from the past, no record of evasion, the end of some ugly chapters. And from here out, until we're manifested on our Freedom Bird, we practice to be more or less sober civilians again. Today," he raised a finger. "Today is the first day of the rest of our lives."

"Aw, one last trip to the latrine, a final writing in the sand," begged Jefferson, who felt the ultimate revelation was about to come him.

"Not for me" insisted Jackson, and he pushed his beer can into the center of the table. "I'm done. It's a pact. I'm taking the oath."

And one by one, they signed on, each for different reasons but sharing an unexpected, common sense of purpose. It didn't matter if they had 42 days left or 167; they were going to initiate meaningful projects as of this moment. The imitation rock 'n' roll bands, imported from the Philippines and Korea, could play the E-5 club without them. The beer would drown the sorrows of losers whose only goal was to get through another day. The imagined intellectual breakthroughs and juvenile erotic fantasies would occupy the brains of those who had given up on hard work and steady application, genuine paths to success.

They stood, some more wobbly than others, and marched toward the door. The Clean Slate Program had begun.

They gave it up, of course, the next night. It was not the first day of the rest of their lives.

Still, the short-lived desire not to disintegrate may have helped them become responsible civilians back in The World. Guilty survivors — though not quite consumed by survivors' guilt — they had to live with the fact that Tract's story ended here and theirs was to be continued.

The Midnight Chopper

Driving west from the St. Louis airport on a hot August afternoon, Mark Landon thought of the state of his life in terms of the condition of his automobile: steady, reliable, economical; but not speedy, surprising, or exciting.

When he heard the thump-thump-thump of a helicopter passing overhead, he recalled the time when the vehicle he once rode in could take him—with surprising speed—into or out of excitement in Vietnam.

The tan Valiant, famous for its sturdy slant-six engine, did have its dents and rattles, its temperamental quirks like stalling during the warm-up period. Some interior light bulbs and control knobs had gone; it wouldn't hold the wheel alignment for long; rust had eaten at places so that, in heavy rain, water leaked through the air vents and dripped on the driver's foot. But the machine always started, and it got Mark and his wife Arabella wherever they wanted to go.

Twenty years earlier he couldn't go anywhere except where the Army told him to go. But today he heard, in memory, Warren Stevens, the itinerant Army reporter, telling him that they could escape their present predicament: "There's always the Midnight Chopper," he said. There had been more mobility then than he recognized at the time.

Stuck at MAC-V in Saigon on his return from R & R in Honolulu, Mark had been told he wouldn't be able to travel until morning, so he wandered off to an enlisted men's club to drink beer and listen to a Filipino band play "Proud Mary" and other favorites of American boys far from home. Warren, on his way out on a story, joined Mark, and they drank to dull their awareness of the fact that neither seemed to have any particular desire to go anywhere.

Today, after dropping his in-laws off at the St. Louis airport, Mark had felt comforted by the stability of his marriage, his profession, and his faith, especially when he passed several cars that had been knocked out by the heat. Their hoods were up on the side of the road, and steam clouded around the heads of their dispirited owners. Somehow he knew his less expensive, less luxurious four-door sedan would run smoothly back to Jefferson City. There was much to be said for such reliability. But there was also, he had come to admit, an odd yearning for the presence of danger.

At a meeting last winter of his church vestry, he had been puzzled by one man's insistence that they pray for "the boys we lost forty years ago." It was D-Day.

"Man, WWII is history," thought Mark. "Can't we get on with life!" Now he wondered if he was going to become one of those veterans who, in old age, found little in life worth remembering except a brief period of (in his case, undesired) wartime military service.

As the traffic thinned beyond the last of the new shopping malls outside St. Louis, Mark did fret that his middle-class, middle-age life was as uninteresting and inconsequential as his automobile. Over the weekend he had been proud to show his visiting parents-in-law the house he and Bella had bought, a three-bedroom rancher with den appropriate by conventional standards to the raising of their five- and nine-year-old children.

Like the agent who sold them the house, he had announced each feature as a special attraction ("spacious den," "full basement," "wooded lot"). But as he pointed them out to Jim and Marsha, they seemed suddenly to turn into restrictions (the family room locked him in front of the television, the workbench heaped chores upon his back, his yard was buried in oak leaves). Squinting down the length of the highway at the western horizon, Mark saw the question rise up before him like a storm cloud: was this how he was going to spend the rest of his life?

Exploring his restlessness in the same way he sometimes looked at the shirts in his closet without knowing why none of them seemed right, he slowed as traffic coming north on Highway 63 merged with cars on Highway 50 headed west to Jefferson City. He was brought up sharply by a sound, a metallic clang, under or within or to the side of the car.

"Uh-oh," he thought and switched off the roaring air conditioner, an add-on unit beneath the dash that just did cool the front seat passengers but left those in back (usually the children, Taylor and Leslie) uncomfortable. The road noise in the aging Valiant was such that, particularly with the air conditioner running, Mark couldn't be sure what he had heard.

Neither he nor Warren could understand what they heard that night in Saigon, where the band's playing was loud and the space small. They had to wait for breaks between songs and between sets to talk. At one point, Warren joked that he and Mark could, if they wanted, leave the club, get over to Ton Son Nhut Air Base, and then take "The Midnight Chopper," a nightly helicopter mail run. As a reporter, Warren had learned all sorts of ways to get around in-country. And he told Mark the route would take him back to his unit before dawn.

"There's always The Midnight Chopper," he repeated, meaning that no situation existed in which two intelligent, educated men couldn't find a way forward. Of course, they both knew they had resources because they were among the privileged clerical class of the Army—enlisted men, but with college education and stateside experience of how the military operates. Grunts had no Midnight Choppers.

Mark's first thought was that a part of the Valiant's engine or drive train had broken loose from its mountings, flung itself out to the grassy ditch on the side of the road. But the car continued to run as steadily as ever. And no parts lay in the road behind him, visible through the rearview mirror. Probably he had heard some sound from the roadside, the blow of a hammer or a door slamming, a crash in someone else's life.

Perhaps what Mark wanted, though, now that he thought about it, was a new crash in life, an event that would cast in sharp relief the forces of history, the shape of the times around him.

The world's major events seemed so distant from where he lived that their effects, like ripples on a lake, thinned to insignificance by the time they reached him. Traveling so far from their source, they became indistinguishable in talk about the election of town officials, debates about zoning, recordings of inches above or below annual rainfall. The connections between his own little world and the life of, say, Washington, D. C., the nation's capitol, were distressingly fragile.

In the capitol of old French Indochina, Mark and Warren left the E-5 club before 9:00 in order to be at the flight pad before the travel curfew. Now they sat side by side on the ground at Tan Son Nhut, legs stretched out before them, backs up against a metal shed. They had decided to gamble on the possibility of a helicopter ride out. Unfortunately, that gave them time, in the shadows of the control tower, to emerge from the comfortable state of numbness they had attained at the club into a new awareness of themselves as unhappy, reluctant soldiers.

From time to time they listened to a disembodied voice over a loudspeaker announcing choppers coming and going. Each represented a potential ride for the dozen or so men trying to get to their destinations that night. But despite the fact that Tan Son Nhut was a center of travel north, south, east, and west, Mark and Warren had been, so far, stranded.

Worried about that clanking sound, Mark decided to pull off and get gas on the outskirts of Jefferson City. While the tank filled, he walked around the car and inspected. Ah, there it is: the right front hubcap was gone. That had been the clanking sound he'd heard. It had slipped loose from the wheel and banged off pavement into the weeds. Shoot! A new hubcap would be costly, and replacing it time consuming. He felt an unwarranted gloom descend on him.

A fog or mist or simply one-hundred-per-cent humidity lay on the ground of Ton Son Nhut Air Base, a palpable atmosphere of moisture. It clouded the night air so there was zero visibility until several hundred feet up. Still, from unexpected, unpredictable directions, helicopters, their searchlights burning, suddenly took shape around them. Their pounding blades drowned out conversation.

In a gap between arrivals and departures, Warren finally shouted that it was too late for to travel that night. The Midnight Chopper must have been scrubbed, and there would be no other ride going his way before daylight. But, for no reason whatsoever, Mark had a feeling they still would escape into the night.

Warren insisted, "Let's get a few hours sleep in a transients barracks. You can find ground transportation in the morning, and I'll get on my way with another bird."

"But there is always a Midnight Chopper," his companion complained, peering up into the darkness.

Then Mark foresaw that he would recover the lost hubcap rather than replace it. There would be a miraculous restoration of his automobile and the status quo. He would get in the car again. He would drive east on the same road he'd just taken. He would ride back on the hot black asphalt, the windows down, his eyes and his senses ready; and the hubcap, the hubcap lying in the grass beside the road, the hubcap would know he was coming and be ready.

The hubcap would, in fact, shift ever so slightly in the grass as he approached (or the wind would nudge it or gravity would have had just enough effect to cause it to sink a few degrees from its past elevation) so that it caught the sun. And as the '75 Valiant approached, the hubcap, which would know its separation and yearn to rejoin the whole, would align itself with higher powers, with the true nature of things, with all celestial bodies, in order to catch a beam of summer light from the afternoon sun.

Yes, a gleam of golden August, the hubcap would catch it and throw it out, out from the grass and the ditch, up through the car window and into his, into Mark's eye, which would be ready, his eye would be prepared for this sign, a sign of cosmic unity that would signal his own ultimate oneness with the universe, his rightful place in the stream of history even at this moment of trouble and doubt. He would go get that hubcap and then make love to his wife!

Make love to your wife. What a goofy thought; where did it come from? He was recalling the old Army joke about the first thing you do when you return home from Vietnam: first, you make love to your wife (though those weren't the exact words you used); then you put down your duffle bag.

Mark remembered, too, how, just after Warren insisted they go to the transients' barracks, down through the fog came the sound of one more arriving aircraft. Then, lights sliced through mist, and the gray-green belly of an Army helicopter descended toward earth. The infamous Midnight Chopper, it turned out, had just been running far behind schedule. (Well, there was a war going on!)

Still, eight soldiers, including Warren and Mark, were waiting for rides when that Huey descended, its motor whining, its blades thumping in the thick night air. And the two of them were the last of the eight in line.

Hueys had space—after their own crew, including pilot, copilot, and door-gunners—for about six passengers. Even if this bird had been empty, there should not have been room for all who were waiting.

That's what the flight control deck initially informed everyone over the loudspeaker, calling out that there was space for three riders. The first troops in line shouldered their gear and walked out to the chopper. The next two grunted and walked back toward the tower and the transients' barracks somewhere beyond it.

That still left one person ahead of Warren and Mark, no seat for him, no possibility of a ride for others. Warren said, "Well, that's it. Let's give it up."

"No, wait."

The hubcap was not waiting for Mark along Route 50, at least as he made the eastward pass. There had been little traffic in the lazy afternoon, the song of his tires on the pavement mixing with the melodies of distant chain saws, tractors, animal calls. But paused at the intersection of 50 and 63, he could only hope he been looking on the wrong side of the road. Too, that hubcap might have rolled who knows how far. So, he turned around, the afternoon sun swinging over the car and now highlighting bright objects ahead of him. Lower in the afternoon sky, too, its rays could bank off roadside objects.

"Now I'll see it," he thought, convinced that the hubcap would appear to him in the next ten minutes.

Just when Mark and Martin were sure all places on the Midnight Chopper were full, the invisible controller, with no explanation, announced that there was room for one more. This guy seemed to have as many seats on this bird as he needed!

The man in front of them gave a jump, grabbed his stuff, and trotted out to get on board. That extra seat shouldn't have been there, and this surely was the end of the night for Warren and Mark.

"There it is," Warren said. "Now let's give it up, go get a few hours sleep, at least, before morning."

Mark caught his arm and said again, "Wait," because now his attention was focused on one of the door-gunners standing beside his ship.

Helicopter crews wore one-piece, olive drab flight suits and round, light-colored helmets. Each helmet had a thin microphone reaching around from the side, by the ear, to rest in front of the mouth. The mics almost touched the crewmembers' lips so that they could communicate while the noisy helicopter (and its weapons) operated.

Mark could see this gunner standing on the tarmac right beside the ship, electrical lines like umbilical cords still linking him to the chopper. But Mark could not see his face because the fog, the night, the distance made only an outline visible. The sphere of the helmet was clear, but the face in the middle was, from his vantage point, in total darkness. Mark looked right at that darkness, that emptiness.

The last man ahead of them had gotten on board. The Midnight Chopper's engine continued to idle; the mist swirled; Warren pulled on his arm. Mark was still looking at this fellow soldier, the door-gunner, standing by his ship.

After perhaps thirty seconds of their staring at each other, the gunner unhooked himself from the ship and started to walk toward him, continuing to gaze directly at Mark. He walked to the edge of the pad, right up to within two feet of Mark and Warren, and leaned forward.

In the light from the tower his face suddenly appeared at the center of his helmet. It was the grinning, freckled face of a nineteen-year-old kid from, it seemed at the time, a small town along Route 66. And he said with a happy smile, "You guys want a ride?"

Apparently, his hubcap had taken a ride off the road, through the bushes, into some dark hiding place. Mark did not see it on the return trip home.

Still, haunted by an unshaken conviction that it was somehow recoverable, he drove back one more time to Nineveh, a community not even big

61

enough to be a village, midway between where he'd heard the sound and where he'd stopped for gas. He followed a gravel road to a country store visible from the highway. Perhaps someone there could give him some help.

Freedman's Little Store, identified by a hand lettered sign over the door, sat so close to the road there was no room for a sidewalk to pass between building and pavement. Evidently, it had once been a single-car garage and the road in front much narrower, allowing for a short driveway. The building's weathered siding matched that of the two-story, turn-of-the-century house sitting farther back and a little higher in the yard. Generous porches with peeling rails reached around three sides of the house, and the roof badly needed to be redone.

The store was more a distribution point than a retail business. Second-hand clothes on metal racks and used kitchen items on unsteady wooden tables took up the tiny space inside. The two large windows facing the road were filled with old framed pictures, rag dolls, household decorations. On the far side of the little store was, unbelievably, a collection of hubcaps, perhaps 75 — perhaps 100, spread out on the grass.

A small black man appeared suddenly at his elbow, perhaps Mr. Freedman himself. He wore dark blue trousers and a white shirt, wire-rimmed glasses. He smiled. "See something you want?"

Well, of course, they wanted a ride! That's what Mark and Warren had been waiting the past three hours for. But how did this boy have a seat for two more on a full bird? How did he know they were holding out beyond all reason and beyond all hope for a place on this chopper?

Nonetheless, he and Warren walked with their newfound friend across the tarmac. They got onto the helicopter, which somehow had two places in the canvas net seating right there by the door, buckled in, and were lifted right up into the night sky by this bosom buddy they had never seen before and would never see again.

Warren and Mark were lifted up into the sky, the Vietnamese night as if by magic, extra passengers who were accommodated on an already full helicopter. The whole sequence of events later reminded Mark of Jesus' disciples on the road to Emmaus, puzzled by how many they were because they didn't recognize the risen Christ among their party.

Mark always recalled that helicopter ride as a spiritual experience. The bird's vertical takeoff, its dip and sweep onto the horizontal, the lift up through and above the fog. The side doors were open as usual (for the gunner at the ready), and Mark was right at the edge, loosely belted to the wall behind him. He felt, for a moment, like an angel rising toward heaven.

"Um, I'm looking for . . . I lost a hubcap." Mark told Mr. Freedman. He turned his bead and gestured. "Tan Valiant. I thought I'd see if I could find anything close."

"Look about yourself," said the proprietor, very friendly.

Mark was a bit disoriented, as he seldom had much interaction with African-Americans. The other highway engineers he worked with were all white; he lived in a white neighborhood, and his children's schools had only a few minority students. He knew Lincoln University was a vital part of the city, but he had never set foot on its campus. The Civil Rights Movement was slow in changing social demographics.

Still, encouraged by the shop owner, he looked back at the hubcaps already on his car so that he could focus on what he was seeking: a solid surface with the imprint of something like a star radiating out from the center, each spoke or ray tapering to a point at the edge of the circle.

On the ground before him was a veritable galaxy of hubcap design, each presumably distinctive to a brand, model, and year. He had never noticed this variety on the cars driving past him, having assumed, if he'd thought about it at all, that there were perhaps three or four basic patterns for all American-made hubcaps. None looked exactly right here, but several seemed close enough to bring him back to their places on the row for a closer examination.

He picked up one, same solid surface but spokes making it resemble a wagon wheel more than a star.

"Take it on over to your car, if you want," said Mr. Freedman, pointing to the Valiant. "See how it looks. Take two or three, as many as you like."

Surveying the hubcaps spread out on the grass like tiles ready to finish a floor, Mark recalled how, on the way to his R & R, he'd come into Saigon by land on an Army transport vehicle. On the outskirts of the city, in places where the war had leveled everything, he saw neighborhoods made up of buildings constructed with flattened American beer cans.

Each can had been opened, the top and bottom removed, and the body hammered into a square. Many squares connected made colorful but not very sturdy or permanent walls, roofs, doors. These Falstaff-Pabst Blue Ribbon-Budweiser buildings housed (if that was the right word) thousands, rather tens of thousands, of refugees who had flooded into the city from the North and from the countryside.

Those shacks, neighborhoods, towns (without electricity of course), were not visible at night from the air. When, with the Midnight Chopper, Mark had soared up into the sky on an imagined or discovered connection with a fellow American, the boyish smiling door-gunner, he had allowed a harsh reality to be obscured by dark and fog from sight and memory.

Many of the lights he saw through gaps in the clouds were from U.S. installations, military and civilian posts. But there was a pattern linking together the darknesses also. Any kinship with humanity Mark had celebrated from above this scene linked mostly Americans, soldiers far from home, their shared country and culture. It excluded those less fortunate on the ground, citizens of this country who had no, and desired no, escape from their homeland.

"Thanks," said Mark, pleasantly surprised at the cheerfulness of the little shop's proprietor, his happiness at helping out a customer.

The man seemed utterly unconcerned about his merchandise. There were no price tags on items here, surely no overall inventory. The few other customers, all black, looked through clothes on racks or wandered inside, chatting among themselves easily, quietly. A few outside simply stood in the shade of the store, taking in the day. Closer to the house, on the grass just behind the display of hubcaps, two children, the age of Mark's daughter or a few years older, were playing.

He could see no other person who might be working for the man he thought of as Mr. Freedman. The little store, a one-man operation, offered a miscellany, things brought together from disparate sources, none terribly valuable, but each serviceable. The owner seemed most concerned that his customers—or at least Mark— find what they wanted. Perhaps if we come down to price, thought Mark, we'll see how the system really works.

When he reached his car, the two hubcaps he carried with him were obviously not identical to the originals. One, in fact, was a different size. (There were different sizes to hubcaps? He'd never known that.) Unfortunately, the one close to the correct pattern was too big for his wheel; the other fit neatly, but was in clear contrast to its mate on the rear wheel.

He went back to the collection again, met by Mr. Freedman. "Find what you want?"

"I'm close. But neither of these is exactly what I need."

"Well, you keep on looking. Sometimes you don't see what you want the first time."

As Mark bent to return the hubcaps to their places in Mr. Freedman's orderly display, he found himself looking directly at a hubcap that seemed remarkably right. Still stooping, he looked back over his shoulder to the car, again at the hubcap lying on the ground before him. How had he missed this one before?

As he straightened and turned to take the new hubcap over to the Valiant, the irrational conviction came over him: this was not just an adequate replacement, not just a generic Chrysler hubcap that would fit with his others. This was the thing itself, his own lost hubcap magically come back to him!

At his car again, he held the new hubcap next to an old one: the same. He positioned it on the front wheel's rim: a perfect fit. A rubber mallet appeared by his right hand, supplied by Mr. Freedman. He knocked the hubcap into place, a firm precise union of cover and rim. He rose flushed, thrilled.

"What do I owe you?," he asked, returning the mallet almost giddily. He only now acknowledged a slight worry, that he might not be carrying enough cash with him. He had no idea what this was going to cost, beyond his wild earlier speculations about requesting a new hubcap all the way from Detroit. He thought he had nearly $40.00 in his wallet, however.

Mr. Freedman looked him steadily in the eyes. "That will be $3.00," he said, smiling brightly.

Mark was flabbergasted, $3.00! A steal, a giveaway. He was embarrassed to find that a $10 bill was the smallest he had. Would Mr. Freedman have change; was there a cash register in this business? Mark wondered. But the storeowner simply excused himself to step inside, return in a moment, and count out carefully ("four, five") the two ones and a five ("and five makes ten"). Done.

Mark thanked him and then found himself wanting to shake his hand, to communicate somehow the extent of the service Mr. Freedman had done him, the degree of his own gratitude. After all, his car, a regular reminder of the crises and failures of daily life, now represented a wholeness so satisfying it was seeping into Mark's outlook on the world.

And Mr. Freedman had done it all at such a generous price. But a handshake seemed excessive for the transaction, so much of its significance private to the buyer. Mark simply said he hoped he'd be back again (which wasn't really true) and turned toward his car.

Even as he faced about, however, his mind ran on ahead with questions. All those hubcaps, how did they get here? Of course, Mark answered himself, Mr. Freedman and his store were known throughout this rural area. Anyone out in the county who found a hubcap sold it to Mr. Freedman, probably for something like a dollar.

But who exactly kept an eye out for lost hubcaps, who walked the roadside ditches for bottles, cans, trash? The poor, that other community in and around Jefferson City about which Mark knew so little.

A set of social connections was highlighted for Mark by the journey of his hubcap — out of white hands through black hands back to him. In his mind he saw a new aerial depiction of the area with two sets of symbols, one marking the (to him) familiar white structure of roads, neighborhoods, government offices; another new set revealing the homes, churches, clubs of the African-American community.

He turned the key, started his car. Checking the rearview mirror for traffic, he eased back onto the road that would take him out to Highway 50 and on to home. Freedman's Little Store receded behind him in the rearview mirror.

He wondered if his recollections of Vietnam were also fading as he moved forward in time. Or were they brightening in such a way that they might obscure his vision of the present? He realized he would have to work harder than he'd ever expected to maintain a proper balance of all the elements of his life. The gut-wrenching reaction to incoming, the domestic hosting of in-laws; a daytime routine of work, nightmare of memory; the celebration of anniversaries and the event of death.

The trusty Valiant did not rise, as a helicopter could, straight up from the scene, offering deliverance from confusion and loss. Instead, it kept him bound to the earth and to the land that defined him as a child and to which he had returned as an adult. No angel yet, ready to rise to heaven but deeply moved, he prayed he could follow a righteous path in a world mixed with plenty and deprivation, characterized by social harmony and lost souls, full of bright sunshine and the dark of midnight.

Who Do You Think Were There?

Knox hadn't seen Butcher for nearly fifty years. They would never have gotten together in Old Salem if they hadn't received the address list Alex Tracy was continually revising for their upcoming high school reunion. The fiftieth would be next year in their hometown of Sikeston, Missouri.

That Gary and Freddy were among the few from the class of '63 who'd migrated east and not west was a factor in their decision to stage a mini-pre-reunion. That they were both Vietnam veterans probably mattered more, though it was unlikely either would have said so initially.

Freddy's wife Barbara asked, "How well did you know Gary growing up." If Gary had had a significant place in her husband's past, he'd kept quiet about it for decades.

"Not that well," he admitted. Then he chuckled, thinking back. "To tell you the truth, I worry that the first thing he'll do is put me in a headlock."

Gary was the fullback on the football team, and little guys like Freddy couldn't do anything if he decided to give one of them the noogies in gym class.

"Good grief, you guys are 67 years old! Surely, you're past that sort of thing." She huffed off to the kitchen to make herself a cup of tea while he reviewed his email in the den.

He knew more than he was telling about Gary but didn't see any reason to share that with Bobby right now. After all, lots of kids who got in trouble as teenagers grew up to be respectable citizens. Running away from home wasn't all that bad, especially in the '60s. And, according to Alex's reunion roster, Gary had received a Bronze Star in Vietnam. Freddy, reserved about his own — unanticipated — overseas service, wondered about the details. They turned out to be illusive, but oddly satisfying.

"What does Butcher do now?" he emailed Alex, the self-appointed reunion coordinator. Freddy had volunteered to help build a class database, so they were determining what information should be included and which omitted — in was military service, out were the number of divorces. (Details about the deceased might be restricted simply because information was missing in many cases.)

"I talked to him on the phone once. He doesn't have email, but I think he told me he's a baker."

Freddy thought of the old rhyme, "the butcher, the baker, the candlestick maker." All that was left for Gary Butcher was the third profession.

Freddy's own recollection also had the infamous headlock king working in the food industry. Around 1973 or '74, Gary had called him out of the blue from Athens, Georgia. Freddy was in graduate school in Atlanta then, and Gary was on his way to a Georgia-Georgia Tech football game. "Wanna' get a beer before the game?" he asked Freddy in a hearty manner, as if they'd done this many a time in many a place.

Freddy, though, was studying for his Ph.D. qualifying exams. And basically a "brain" in high school, he'd never been friends with Gary, a prominent school figure (if sometimes for the wrong reasons). He wants to have a beer with me? Freddy politely declined.

Forty years later he had a pang of guilt when, recalling his hesitancy in that conversation, he learned how close Gary was to where he lived now. Why not offer to make it up, since he and Bobby had already planned the trip to Winston-Salem?

He did recall Gary back in high school coming into Sikeston's better pool hall, The Cellar, which served no booze, allowed women (few came), and let the pot-bellied WWII veterans establish proper behavior by example. Half a dozen of them, cigars clamped in their teeth, regularly leaned over the three-rail billiard and snooker tables up front, sometimes alluding quietly to war stories known only to each other. Freddy used to stop in before or after his soda jerk job at Downtown Drugs to apply the rules of geometry in a practical arena.

Gary was often at the Cellar's challenge table (two players put up a dime each; the winner pocketed the other's coin and played the owner of the next dime placed along the rail). Tiring of taking everyone's money, he might wander around the other tables and choose a victim for his headlock. Freddy could remember the helpless feeling of his head imprisoned by that huge arm.

He imagined Gary now with the traditional chef's hat, a large white apron covering a significant gut. Perhaps he struggled to keep up with the physical demands of kneading dough, making bread, cake, and pies in the same way Freddy battled difficult new computer programs.

"If you do see Gary," Alex's email concluded, "ask him why he kept the ball from me so much." He followed his joke with the email shorthand for a smile: :). Alex had been the basketball team's center and Gary, the good all around athlete, a forward.

Alex hoped Gary would come to their fiftieth reunion because, captain of the football team, he could dance again with Ellen Montgomery, homecoming queen. It would be one more note of nostalgia, a gesture toward their former innocence—pre-Sexual Revolution, pre-Vietnam, pre-Watergate. But for some reason, Alex seemed to think it unwise to ask Gary up front if he would reenact homecoming. Freddy was to sound him out gently, keeping this goal of the visit to himself until he could determine how Gary might respond.

Alex's reticence reinforced Freddy's feeling that there was more to Gary's past—both in high school and after—that Alex worried might keep him away from the reunion. Freddy also wondered if Alex held some private ideas about where he, a former nerd, belonged in the class of '63. He might well have thought Freddy the last person to take an active part in the event planning or to make a special effort to contact Gary.

Freddy had been pretty much a loner in high school and now was professor emeritus of mathematics at the University of Virginia, a theorist whose work was of interest to only a handful of other specialists around the world. After those two years as an Army draftee, he had lived in a realm of abstraction. Gary, however, had always been a hands-on person: gripping the football, closing a headlock, squeezing the girls.

But there he was, immediately recognizable (Freddy had studied the old yearbook picture in advance), standing in the foyer of Blackbeard's Hideout, an obviously popular Sunday brunch spot in Winston-Salem.

"I hope you're Gary Butcher," Freddy said, extended a hand, not certain he wouldn't still have to dodge a headlock.

Gary skipped the handshake and instead embraced him warmly. "And you're Freddy Knox, haven't changed a bit." He released Freddy and shook Barbara's hand, escorting them in to where Nancy, his wife of forty-six years, held a table. Still a big man, he looked reasonably trim and fit, though, interestingly, Freddy found himself only a little shorter now. He had gotten his height late.

They were all causally dressed, but Freddy thought the Butchers' clothes more expensive and stylish than his own. The couple were also relaxed, apparently used to such social situations, though Gary's hands played over the table from time to time in a restless manner.

Freddy's wife, who had wanted to see Old Salem for a long time, fell into an immediate conversation with Nancy about that little community. A minister herself, Gary's wife knew all about the 18th-century Moravian settlement buried in the heart of the current Winston-Salem, a city of over a quarter of a million people. Nancy offered to show Bobby the craft shops, take her to the old church, and explain the seldom-told history of religious persecution that drove these Christians out of Europe to the New World. Freddy never imagined what he would learn today about the past—the world's, Gary's, and his own.

The Knoxes had a good marriage, but, of course, they kept some secrets from each other, mostly concerning their childhoods, when everyone is vulnerable and so much is unknown. To a large degree, though, they no longer cared what skeletons hid in their closets. Ghosts couldn't scare away the proven commitment to each other, to children, to community.

Barbara had waited for him when he went overseas, and Freddy felt even a life of faithfulness could never equal her sacrifice in following an enlisted man to Tennessee and then waiting that year back home. The spouses of soldiers who lived apart from the military community, especially those in academia, encountered the anger of anti-war sentiment and sometimes even chose to withhold information about their absent husbands. Bobby would learn Nancy had endured a similar situation studying religion as an undergraduate while Gary was on the other side of the world.

Gary recommended the house's brunch special, Baked Pecan French Toast, but said, patting his stomach, he'd have his without the syrup. After their orders—four of the special— were taken, Freddy said to Gary, "Alex writes that you're a baker. How did that happen?"

Gary laughed. "The Army." He went on, his hands again moving over the table as if affirming the order of things. "When I went in . . . you know how they give you all those tests, to see what you're good at? Well, they found I had defective vision, one tiny blind spot, a minuscule dot on this retina." He pointed to his right eye. "They informed me I was not combat material."

"That was lucky!"

"That's what I thought at the time, but there are other things they don't tell you, especially about what can happen in wartime. So, anyway, when they went over all my scores and things, they told me I could be a chef, a baker, or a butcher. It turns out they saw abilities in me I'd never suspected. Anyway, without thinking, I said 'baker.'"

"And that's it?"

"Yes, and no. Eight months later I was riding shotgun on convoys in and out of Bien Hoa. Things were hot now and then, but not from any oven! Every time I got back, I'd report to my CO: 'Major Johnson, Sir! Private Gary Butcher, Sir!'" Gary paused and grinned, opening his hands, a gesture of mock bewilderment. "'Sir, I'm a baker!'"

Freddy laughed, too, aware that this was not an insignificant act in the military of that day, when enlisted men simply followed orders without pointing out contradictions. "It didn't work, did it?"

"Not right away, but at some point, I actually did get transferred, down to Vung Tau. And I went back to baking."

"Good for you! I heard that was a good place to be, a private resort city for the French, wasn't it?"

"And a great tourist spot today, I'm told, not that I ever want to vacation there."

Freddy wasn't one of those vets who wanted to go back and tour the place he'd been stationed either. But, hearing Gary's account, he suspected something was being left out. You couldn't request a transfer and get it that easily, even if your current assignment called for skills you didn't possess. For much of the remainder of their conversation Freddy searched the back of his mind for a memory he couldn't quite pull up out of the darkness.

"Where were you stationed?" Gary asked, and Freddy gave a succinct account of his monotonous days as a signal support systems specialist at Cam Rahn Bay, leaving out, of course, the steady drinking, occasional pot, a few porno film viewings. He had no horrors of combat to conceal beyond occasional rockets that chose to avoid wherever he happened to be.

Later, while they waited for their food, he asked Gary if he was still a baker. "Retired seven years ago. I'd done so much travel, I woke up one morning and couldn't remember which state I was in. I called Nancy, and all she could tell me was that I was not in North Carolina."

"So, you didn't stay with a single bakery for your whole career, then?"

"Oh, no. Things happened." He moved the silverware in front of him, making the arrangement neat and then redoing it. "The first job I had was in New York City. They recruited me from the vocational school I went to outside of Chicago—paid for the by the GI Bill, of course— and the money looked so good, I didn't study the fine print."

"Hidden clauses?"

"Let's put it this way: I found out I was in charge of one hundred employees, and only two had a word of English. It was a nightmare."

Freddy compared this to his own work where mathematics was a shared and precise language, no matter what country you came from. You even agreed on the unknowns!

"I made it through that year, but Nancy and I wanted to get out of the North. That's how we ended up down in Georgia in the '70s."

"Right. I've always regretted not being able to get away that Saturday . . . a busy time . . ."

"I know how it is, especially when you're getting started." They were both lost in thought for a few moments, the pleasures of retirement obvious. Freddy realized that Nancy and Bobby had been as engaged in talk as he and Gary, finding kinship in their generation, their delayed professional careers, their children.

As the food was being served, he asked Gary, "So, you still bake? You know, for yourself, for Nancy?"

"Not really. Well, now and then maybe a cake for a special occasion. But people generally can't imagine the kind of baking I did when I was in a kitchen. We're talking about 1,000 pounds of dough for starters."

"Ah, I see what you mean. I could do the calculations but never connect what I watch Bobby doing in the kitchen to the large machines you probably used."

"The calculations were the hard part for me," laughed Gary. "A gap in my education I was clever at covering up for a long time."

They all turned to the French Toast for a few moments. Then Freddy asked, "Why did you pick Winston-Salem for your retirement?"

"Well, the company moved me here a dozen years ago. We were always getting bought up by larger and larger corporations, transferred from city to state by Sara Lee at one point, then a Germany company, even a multinational firm toward the end. Sometimes we had felt our bosses were invisible, stationed in a country we'd never heard of and couldn't find on any map of the world."

Freddy realized his classmate had to have been successful, never losing his position through all those changes and able to retire in his 50s. He must have been promoted into management, not exactly the career one would forecast from his rowdy school days.

"That's funny. I got my first teaching job in Virginia, and thirty-five years later I'm still there—retired, of course, though I keep an office for research purposes."

A story he'd heard at Cam Rahn Bay seemed to be surfacing from the past, something about a convoy ambush. What was it?

"We like it in North Carolina," Gary observed. "And, as it turned out, I had family in the area, an uncle who retired to Columbia, South Carolina. He was developing Alzheimer's, and I started going down to help him. He had no children."

Gary had lost his father when he was a child, five or six. In those days, it would have been hard for a single parent like his mother, because widows didn't fill out the blanks on social calendars of the orderly middle class. Mrs. Butcher never remarried and lived alone. Years later, her son took on the care of an uncle who was being lost to disease.

"Alzheimer's is hard," Freddy admitted. "They're there but not there."

"Yes. But there was no one else to help. And at the end, he left me his house. Our daughter's there now, so it's staying in the family."

As they reviewed more family history, Freddy learned that Gary also chose early retirement in order to let his wife devote herself to her career (she was an Episcopal priest with, he claimed, "a gift for finding lost sheep") and to help babysit the grandchildren. Their son taught at a school for those troubled kids that regular schools lacked the capacity — or the patience — to handle.

That made Freddy remember how Gary had been suspended from high school for a month in his senior year—fortunately after football season. He'd gotten in a fight with a boy from a rival school and then disappeared for two weeks. His mother had been frantic, and the whole town was alerted to look for any sign.

It turned out Gary had been camping out in a cave just beyond the city limits, sometimes wearing a disguise and walking into the Kroger's to shoplift food he slipped beneath his sweatshirt. He'd been right under their noses all along, but when he happened to see his mother disappearing into Downtown Drugs—but not before he caught the lost look on her face—he turned himself in.

Gary would never say what had caused the fight, though a rumor grew that the other boy had said something about Mrs. Butcher's secret love life. Of course, there was none. The exact words used were ones you kept out of your speech whenever girls were present in that era; and they could frequently lead to blows. Freddy, who knew none of these details at the time but was close to both his mother and father, had wondered then how anyone could hurt his parents.

"Your children are close?" he asked Gary.

"Well, the daughter in Columbia, and the son in Raleigh." He smiled at his wife, who was listening. "Nancy likes to keep an eye on them, even though they're both in their thirties. And there are three grandchildren." Nancy raised her eyebrows at him, a sign Freddy understood to mean Gary might be the one who enjoyed his family being close.

"Well, you and I are not far apart, Gary, so why don't you come up and see us in Virginia?"

"Yes," Bobby agreed. "Monticello is worth going to more than once. I always find something I've overlooked no matter how many times I've been."

And they left it that they would be in touch. Nancy had email, which would make it easy to communicate. Listening to Gary's account of his career made Freddy suspect he had email also, but wanted to keep himself off too many address lists. Freddy had developed his own filters to compartmentalize messages.

Driving north to Virginia, the story came back to him: "The Cooking Oil Quarterback." He had noticed it then because the central figure had been described as "from Missouri" and, in the tired old cliché, as someone who said, "Show me!"

A small convoy had been ambushed on a muddy road west of Cu Chi, and the drivers and support were pinned down for hours before reinforcements could make their way to them. The Americans drove back the NVA and VC in an initial firefight, but that depleted their ammunition and they feared any second assault

84

by a larger force would override their hastily constructed defenses.

One of the men, identified as "a cook hitching a ride on a transport vehicle," rigged some sort of ad hoc fire bombs with cans of cooking oil and fuses made from box twine. When the expected second attack began, according to the account Freddy remembered, the cook resembled the Cardinal's Charley Johnson finding the weak spots in the Packers' defense. The cook poking string into cans of oil was a candlestick maker!

"You know, Gary didn't seem like the kind of boy who would put other boys in headlocks," Bobby commented. "He's so . . . so mild mannered, and said such nice things, worrying about his mother." Mrs. Butcher was in her 90s, still living in Sikeston at an assisted care facility.

"We're all nice guys," explained Freddy.

"You know I didn't mean that."

"I guess we all do grow up, but I promise you, the Gary I knew was a bit different than the retired baker you met today."

The conversation went on to both couples' retirement, to Nancy's delayed college career followed much later by seminary, to shared understanding of the donut holes in long-term health care insurance. Freddy wondered if Gary ever told the story of how, in a sense, he became a "candlestick-maker."

He remembered what a colleague in the anthropology department once told him about "who had gone to the fair" in "Three Maids in a Tub." According to her, the original folk version was aimed at supposedly respectable trades people caught peeking at naked fairground ladies taking a bath. "Who do you think were there?" the storyteller was reporting to his friends with a snicker—"rub-a-dub dub! the butcher, baker, and the candlestick-maker."

Over the next few days, Freddy began to ask himself how cooking oil came to be on that convoy, which had been described, he thought, as a resupply mission for small military outposts along the way. They needed cooking oil out in the bush instead of the standard C-Rations? Wouldn't that go to big bases with mess halls and full staffs?

He was unable to find the original story or anything like it online or at the university library and concluded, sadly, that "The Cooking Oil Quarterback" had been dropped from the official annals of history. One newspaper account, however, led him to speculate. Some GI's, he read, became involved with local populations and occasionally passed on material—not arms, of course—when they had more than they needed for their own operations. Cooks especially—and Freddy thought, bakers—could begin to feel for the hungry villagers, if they got to know them.

Some weeks later, having received a note from Gary about his reunion intentions, Freddy renewed the invitation for the Butchers to come to Charlottesville, hoping the four of them could fill out the story of their journeys from the fair of their youth.

~~~

Fountain

I.

It had been Patty's treasured coming of age story, though it bothered Ray whenever she told even an edited version (omitting the part where he put on the condom). She felt it was a tale of their generation—sweet, profound, generous; transformational, innocent, poignant. But decades later, she feared that both the before and the after of that summer romantic encounter belonged to another world entirely. Ray had finally told her what happened in Vietnam.

At sixty-five, he was stepping down as Registrar at Fontbonne University and brooding about what thirty years of teaching and administrative work really meant. There was to be the public celebration, at which he would try to sum up the value of his career in education. But Patricia wanted a private one as well, an endorsement of their forty year marriage, their fifty year journey from childhood sweethearts to grandparents of three. She was determined to integrate even that horrific experience on Tu Do Street into the tapestry of their personal history together.

"Lately, I really wonder," he told her. "The criticism of universities has been more and more intense. It's as if the country is giving up on the connection between democracy as a form of government and the education of its voters. We're no longer bound together by common interests."

She agreed, but insisted, "What they say about public schools and teachers is even worse." She had taught nursing at St. Louis University Hospital for as long as he had been Fontbonne. "We have to fight the good fight as long as we can."

Then she regretted using the word "fight." She realized the story of massacre, once told, was bothering Ray more and more, rather than finally achieving assimilation. Still, she believed her "show me" narrative had such power that, if revised appropriately, it could put even that event in context. So, while Raymond prepared remarks for his upcoming talk, Patty contemplated ways to rescue their innocence from the past without ignoring the events he had kept from her for forty years.

She began at the beginning.

II.

Reaching a hand into the pocket of her sun dress as she walked across campus, fifteen-year-old Patty Morrow touched the thing she carried to surprise Ray Fuller. The cool plastic hardness of the case, as she curled her fingers around it, was almost a shock to her, though she had put it there herself only a few hours earlier.

Patty wondered what Ray would be bringing to this rendezvous. At the time of his challenge, two days earlier, he had only raised an eyebrow and said he had a "surprise" to show her.

"Is it larger than a bread box?" she had asked innocently, willing to guess within the rules of familiar games.

"You'll see, you'll see. Friday night." According to Patty's understanding of "Twenty Questions," he should have said either "yes" or "no."

Then Ray asked, "What do you have that I don't know about?"

"Me?" she wondered.

So many things were new for these two people emerging into adulthood that each could easily have been surprised by a number of novelties, tricked by questions and answers previously outside the rules they knew. The times in which they lived, the 1950s, were, they would later insist, modern America's Age of Innocence. Thus, they stood on the threshold of individual and collective discovery, the world they knew about to be reconfigured if not exploded.

At first Patty had felt uneasy in this unconventional version of "Show and Tell," aware of the need to identify motives as well as objects. But, as was often the case in her experience, she gained unexpected confidence as time passed.

III.

For the first six months of his Vietnam tour, Ray—then, like Patty, twenty-two—sent back glowing letters about his good fortune: assigned to be a military liaison for the University of Maryland's extension program in Saigon, South Vietnam, and housed in an old French villa less than a mile from the famous Continental Palace Hotel on Tu Do Street. He worked an eight-to-five day as a guidance counselor for service men, identifying military training and experience that could count for college credit and constructing schedules to complete degree programs. It was in harmony with his civilian plans before and after his own tour.

The villa had a staff of South Vietnamese maids and a cook, their own laundry service, and round-the-clock security provided by MPs attached to MAC-V. Except on those increasingly rare occasions when rockets reached the city or suicidal snipers opened fire from the backs of motorcycles, Ray felt it was remarkably like his undergraduate days at St. Louis University.

That Ray had left one institution of learning in the States to work for another in Southeast Asia and then returned to spend nearly all of his career at a third would be the framework on which Patty would construct her tale.

IV.

Approaching the 10:00 p.m. meeting place chosen by Ray, the teenage Patty noticed that the lights around the fountain and the fountain itself had been turned off. She wondered if he had arranged shadows and near silence as well as time and place—a carefully staged event.

Few regular students were taking classes in the summer of 1961 so the campus in general was quiet. Patty could hear automobile traffic moving lazily on streets several blocks away and even, at times, cattle calling from the School of Agriculture fields on the edge of town. Columbia was still a small town, the university, linked, to a degree that now seems rather fantastic, with a fading rural way of life.

Then she saw Ray rise from the fountain's rim, a two-foot-high, brick wall. At the center of the shallow pool near the heart of the university, a single powerful jet of water ordinarily shot perhaps twenty-five feet into the air. Red, blue, and yellow spotlights beamed through the splintering column to create moving shapes, sometimes a rainbow.

"The future!" Patty had thought to herself when she first saw it, just ten days ago.

She, Raymond, and two dozen other high school students from across the state had come to Columbia for The Show Me Institute, which was aimed at encouraging Missouri's best college prospects to apply to the state university. Rising juniors, they had been chosen by their home districts as possessing high academic promise. These bright lights of tomorrow would stay on campus for two weeks, attend special classes, and find out about the university's forward-looking programs. No one at that time, of course, could have predicted the individual dropouts that would accompany broad social upheavals in the next decade, the troubled '60s.

The Show Me Institute may have been designed to promote state education, but, for the young people selected to attend, the two-week residency contained the obvious prospect of summer romance. And dark-eyed Ray Fuller had been marked early by the girls as one to watch, a wolf, they thought, surveying his flock of sheep. It was a role, however, Ray only attempted to play — and, in the end, not successfully.

V.

There was one more school Patty had to connect to their parallel teaching careers: the international school on Tu Do Street. Among Ray's regular recreational activities in Saigon was watching young Vietnamese girls walk to and from that institution still run by an order of French nuns who had stayed behind when most of their countrymen returned home.

Students took courses in European history, the Catholic religion, American culture. They learned

French and English, studied Western music, and hoped to achieve the distinctions that would take them to the Sorbonne, Oxford, or Harvard. One day they would be ready to assist in the development of the new democratic, liberated Vietnam.

Although Western dress had become increasingly popular with Vietnamese women, the required uniform for these girls was the traditional white Áo Dài—a tight-fitting silk tunic worn over pantaloons. Ray associated the clean, simple Áo Dài with virginal femininity, a jewel to be valued and protected.

Raised a strict Baptist, he had been taught to fear Catholics, who, he was told, worshipped idols and the Pope. He came to wonder, though, if that Old World religion might have been able to preserve a principle of chastity under assault at this time. Corporal Trunk's reports of sexual exploits back home and in Saigon regularly reminded him of that unpleasant side of progress.

"Look at that sweet meat," said the corporal, whose job was typing and filing transcripts and other records. He did it poorly. "Wouldn't you like to get into those slinky white pants, GI?" He rubbed his crotch.

Ray blocked such thoughts from his mind. He was still a virgin, committed to abstinence before marriage, even more so after the shameful fountain episode at the University of Missouri. But he was drawn to the beauty of the Vietnamese students' slender forms, their jet black, straight hair done simply, their markedly clear complexions. The way they held hands, laughed with unaffected joy, and traveled together in tight groups inspired his belief that they represented a clean, bright future for the country—once, of course, the present conflict was over.

VI.

Coming to the fountain, the young Patty took in the attractive form of her fellow student: perhaps an inch more than six feet tall, slender and a bit stooped, with the short haircut of the times, Ray represented just the kind of boy Patty might have envisioned in her future beyond high school.

Back home in West Plains, she had been too reserved to draw attention and not yet particularly interested in boys. But the effects of a final, unexpected growth spurt through the spring—it would propel her in another year to the status of a willowy, seemingly aloof young woman—and the sense of a fresh start created by a new place had caused Patty to stand out even among other polished and poised Show Me Institute participants. And she received the invitation from Ray as if it were expected. He asked her after an afternoon lecture by a renowned politics professor.

"The present state of the world is threatening the very existence of freedom," Dr. Bliss explained. "Either brave men of the West will continue to confront the march of godless Communism around the globe, or America's women and children will fall under the domination of the heirs of Stalin."

"Blah-blah-blah," thought Patty, who cared little for politics then.

"Friday night is threatening for me," Ray said to her following the talk.

"Umm? Friday?"

"If you don't meet me, I can't say what I might do."

"Well, I . . . ."

"Ten o'clock. The fountain."

"We aren't supposed to . . . ."

VII.

Not only did Ray's opinion of Catholicism shift during his tour, so did his understanding of career members of the military, especially enlisted men like Sgt. Paul Stillwater.

"Look, man," he told Ray earnestly at their first meeting. "I've been in nineteen years, and I plan to get out at twenty. I was busted back in rank twice, when I was still . . . uh, growing up, so my pension at E-5 ain't going to be that big."

Ray nodded. "I understand. You need to have a degree to get ahead in the civilian world. Let's seen what we can do."

Stillwater's transcript was a hodgepodge of community college offerings, extension classes taught on stateside bases, correspondence courses from universities Ray had never heard of. His grades were generally at a C level, or "pass" in a pass-fail system.

"I got three kids, you know," Paul told him, "two getting ready to finish high school. I wouldn't want them to join up right now," he gestured to the outside. Ray would later learn he'd served his first six months in the boonies, searching and destroying. "Even if they're interested, which they ain't—no dice. But I need to earn enough to help them go to technical school or somethin'."

"Right. Well, you know you can take courses here, when you're off duty. And some of . . . of what you've done can add up toward an associate's degree. Let me, um, compile all your . . . your records and . . . and you come back in a few days. How about that?"

"Thanks, man. I got to put the pieces together, you know? The wife, she's not so happy. When I'm gone, she has to do everything. And teenage boys . . . well, I'm a living example of how they ain't easy to manage. So, like, like I say, I want to build up a better life, take what we got but put more good stuff in it, you know?"

VIII.

Ray's dare for his attractive Show Me Institute fellow — to bring something to surprise each other — came after his plea to meet him at the fountain. And Patty guessed quickly what he would bring.

At their rendezvous, he admitted, "I wasn't sure you'd be here." He sat down again and looked back the way she had come. Both boys and girls, who stayed in separate dormitories on opposite sides of the campus, had strict curfews.

She sat down and looked directly at him. "Well, here we are!" Patty knew he took responsibility for their being here: he was breaking the rules, she only following his lead.

He laid a hand gently on top of hers where it rested on the brick wall, still faintly warm from the evening sun of a long twilight. She did not pull back.

"How did you escape the guards," he said conspiratorially. "I rolled up two extra pillows to look like a person sleeping in bed — another me."

"Oh, what a good idea! I never would have thought of that."

"Our Residence Advisor probably won't even notice."

"What if someone pulls the covers back?"

"My roommate, Billy, agreed to be on the lookout. He'll say I'm sleeping, don't wake me. They'll buy it that I need the rest after our rigorous day, if there's any question. How'd you get away."

"Oh, me? I just walked out the front door."

"No one stopped you?"

"Nope. Some of the other girls might have seen me do it. But I don't know about the R.A.'s."

"That was bold!"

"I guess I figured they wouldn't really expect it of the girls. And I can just say, 'Silly me! — I forgot we were supposed to stay in. Oops!'"

"Hmm. Say, how did you like that biology filmstrip this morning?" The film had been an overview of current scientific research, some of it conducted at Mizzou. There had been predictable tittering at the rabbit pairs used in reproduction experiments.

"Fine. I like animals." She remembered more the men in white lab coats who studied new crops to be farmed on the oceans' floors, futuristic versions of her father who tilled one hundred acres on land originally cleared by his grandfather.

"But would you like to be one of those rabbits, cooped up and watched all the time?" Patty recalled from the film other scientists in dark suits caging Asian predators that could be used to eliminate local pests on the other side of the globe.

"Maybe we're the subjects of an experiment, the 'Show Me Laboratory,'" she joked. This surprised Ray a moment, but he turned it nicely.

"Well, for right now, at least, I think we've escaped from our cages. We can do whatever we want."

This time her directness was more unexpected. "What do you want to do?"

Again, he rebounded, squeezing her hand and turning toward her. "What do you think I want?"

Patty was still partly reviewing the filmstrip in memory. She recalled men wearing stethoscopes who manipulated hormones to amplify growth, strength, even intelligence in controlled populations.

"You want to push back the frontiers," she said slowly, ". . . of science."

IX.

When Ray met Patty for R & R in Hawaii, he was still marveling at his safe duty, so many days steadily marked off his short-timer calendar, plus the genuine service he provided.

"It's like my first real job, honey," he explained. "I'm getting all this experience and learning things, too. It turns out I'm a good listener — or at least, that's what many of the men tell me. I take it all in."

She would have liked him to listen a bit more to what she had to say. Back home with her family, she'd had to endure the outrage of neighbors and family members who couldn't ignore the anti-war protesters, even when many of them had sons or brothers who'd found ways to avoid the draft.

"That's wonderful, dear," she said. "When you get back, we can pick up where we left off, the wedding and then graduate school for you."

Their romance had not really begun at the fountain. She had been put off by his behavior, and he'd been embarrassed. Three years later, when they were students at neighboring schools in St. Louis, she had come to see the incident as amusing, youthful, impetuous. Recognizing him at Fontbonne sorority mixer, she initiated the renewed contact. Engaged in Hawaii, they stayed in separate rooms.

"But, you see, it'll be more than 'picking up.' Just like I said, I've already got better credentials from this job, so I'm going to get my degree in higher education administration. I've already written to three universities and have a foot locker filling up with application material."

As he talked, he was scanning the mountaintop view of the ocean with his new Pentax camera, bought for a very low price at the MAC-V PX. He'd gotten all the lenses and was

101

determined to fill up a scrapbook of his year in Saigon. Here, he'd taken pictures of Diamond Head, the USS Arizona Memorial, the hotel's luau events. He should show it to children and grandchildren.

The photographic record of his time in Vietnam, however, was never shared. He uncovered the Army album only when, approaching retirement, he was searching for a storage place to put boxes from the Fontbonne office. The scrapbook had been packed up with material saved from high school and college. He knew that he had stopped taking photographs abruptly at end of his tenth month in-country.

X.

Almost all the Show Me participants felt their two weeks at the University of Missouri involved a speeding up of experience, chances to race ahead of timetables set for them by others. Patty knew that things were accelerating this summer, but she had maintained her characteristic calm.

At the fountain Raymond turned to her, leaned down. She accepted his kiss, the first truly romantic embrace of her life. She could feel his pleasure, at the contact and at the willingness it revealed. He probably did not sense her control.

Inattentive friends and relatives often mistook her self-confidence for shyness or slowness. She had a knack for timing and seemed to operate on an infallible inner clock, which routinely kept her from accidents, prompted her to action at the right moment.

"That was nice," observed Ray. "Let's do it again." This time he put his long arms completely around her, tilting her head back into the crook of his elbow. Again, she did not resist. But she did not put her arms all the way around him either, instead resting a hand on each of his shoulders.

Ray's left hand came up from Patty's waist to brush against her breast. His breathing was heavy. He would later confess this was completely out of character, an impulse he had not anticipated and could not control.

Unlike most teenagers, who eagerly pressed for new experiences, Patty possessed a certainty that all would come to her in time. Her mother had worried when Patty passed a fourteenth birthday without beginning to menstruate. But the teenager shrugged off concern, assuming that the capacity to bear children was bound to be hers one day. She had had her period for several months before her mother even knew.

She came up for air. "What do you have to show me?" Her own breathing was still even, though she had enjoyed the feel of his lips, the strength of his arm.

Ray paused, and he then smiled, a slightly crooked grin. He exhaled sharply, "Whff!" and reached for his billfold.

XI.

On their last day in Hawaii, Ray told Patty, "I need your measurements."

"Measurements?"

"It's a surprise, something I . . . found. You'll like it."

They were riding in a cab to a restaurant famous for a menu that reflected the many cultural traditions of the islands — Polynesian, British, Asian, American. Out of the window could be seen high-class fashion shops with mannequins wearing the latest styles. She decided he was probably considering a tropical outfit, perhaps a grass skirt and colorful blouse she could wear on special occasions in the future.

"Okay, but I might not always stay this size, you know."

"We're both going to stay just the way we are and never grow a day older. The next four months are going to fly past, and we'll be together forever."

"It will be right at the end of my teaching year. I don't even need to go on a honeymoon so long as you come home safely."

She had always been less able than he to minimize the danger of being in a war zone. She watched the news on all three networks and kept a mental tabulation of the growing U.S. casualties.

She even saved maps that identified reportedly shrinking enemy strongholds and growing areas of pacification. It all added up to a disaster in her mind.

"I just hope you'll be able to get on the plane with all the presents we've bought!" They had come to Honolulu in December and were using the opportunity to shop for Christmas presents. She'd come with a list, and together they'd added more items. They would ship one box home, but everything she could take on the plane would save money.

"The airlines are so nice to all the wives and girlfriends. They'll find a way." Indeed, the Christmas season inspired stewardesses and baggage personnel to wave as many of the rules as they could.

On the flight out, most family members had been almost giddy with excitement, but the return trip was sobering. Patty didn't know how tense she was until she had to use the throw-up bag stored in the seat pocket ahead of her.

XII.

The term "rubber" was not used publicly at the time of the Show Me Institute. Adults might refer vaguely to "prophylactics" (assuming, among other things, that such a scientific sounding term would not be understood by "the ladies"). And "condom" would wait another thirty years before

AIDS provided it with respectability, even dignity. From her brother's friends Patty had learned what rubbers were for: not the prevention of disease, of course, but the prevention of pregnancy.

What Ray thought he was going to do with the rubber he pulled — "Whff!" — from his billfold was never clear even in his own mind. It was all some sort of rash effort to be someone he had never been back home, to have a story to tell, though he hadn't composed an ending.

Patty understood well that in her middle-class, small-town circle, pregnancy before marriage was fatal to individual and family character, no matter what church you attended. Gonorrhea and syphilis (known generally only by the inclusive initials "V.D.") were conditions afflicting older men in big cities, perhaps veterans of foreign military campaigns. In post-World War II middle-America, girls believed in and knew to value their virginity.

For that very reason, an illicit rendezvous at the university fountain with a member of the opposite sex could represent by itself a threat to the rest of Patty's life. But once again, her unerring timing had given her an escape from danger.

"I know what that is," Patty said when, on the fountain's rim, he pulled the square foil packet out of his wallet. "Is it ribbed or tipped?"

The packet, as he held it up, seemed to quiver in the night air.

XIII.

Six weeks before he was supposed to leave Vietnam, Ray's letters stopped. When a second week went past with no letter, Patty began to panic.

"If anything has happened—and I know it hasn't—," her mother insisted, "you would have heard. It's not like earlier wars, where word from the front took weeks to reach home. You're more connected to Ray than your uncle ever was to us."

Uncle Henry had served "for the duration" in World War II, landing on Normandy and marching with his unit all the way to Berlin. He was the source, illogically, of Mrs. Morrow's conviction that nothing would ever happen to anyone in her family during wartime.

"I know, I know," Patty agreed. "But he could call, if there's some reason he can't write or letters aren't being delivered."

Not long after their R & R together, she had had one unsatisfactory, two-minute conversation with Ray via MARS, a telephone-to-amateur radio-to-telephone relay system linking hemispheres. Personal conversations, though, were subject to interruption for higher priority traffic, and sunspots or weather could break up

107

transmission. She had been taken by surprise at six in the morning. She never knew what time of day it had been for him.

Then a package arrived, though it must have taken weeks to get there because it had come by surface transport. "It's the outfit he bought me in Hawaii," concluded Patty, thinking perhaps it should be saved until he was home. She opened it nonetheless.

"To my one true love," the card said, "who will be able to wear this forever." It was a white Áo Dài, tailored in Saigon.

She packed it back carefully, wondering when or on what occasions he envisioned her wearing it.

Then a terse letter came: he was fine, would be home in three weeks, not to worry.

XIV.

Patty had been one of three girls not to head for the Home Economics building when the Show Me Institute choice of tours was offered. Most of the boys visited the engineering departments, but Patty and two others joined the group escorted to the university medical school. She was quick to notice that the administrator's eyes kept coming back to the girls when his gaze swept across the small sea of faces listening to an itemization of the school's up-to-date equipment and training. It might even have been that the itinerary was altered to avoid some planned stops, particularly in the anatomy department.

A decade later she would share with friends the legendary (perhaps apocryphal) story about how men tried to discourage women in medical school. Into the lab coat pocket of the class's one female student, male colleagues slipped a penis, callously obtained from one of the corpses used in anatomy. They assumed the discovery her hand would make during daily rounds sufficient to drive her from the profession.

Their assurance was strained, however, as she went several hours without a sign of discomfort. They saw a hand go deep into that pocket, but it came out again with only a pencil. There was no agitated reaction. And she continued to take rigorous notes on a clipboard.

Some of the men concluded silently that she had freaked out, been shocked into denial. But in the changing room where lab coats were hung on wooden pegs, she threw out a question for the rest of them. Holding aloft the anonymous, inert manhood, she asked casually, "Did one of you boys lose something?"

Patty found the medical school presentations to Show Me Institute kids interesting, the science nicely framed at times in larger contexts of value.

"If you're thinking of a future career in medicine," said Dean Daily, "you will have to be a good student and a kind teacher. You must learn to tell your patients and their families what you're prescribing and why."

"What about research positions or specialties?" asked Samuel, a declared pre-med from Independence with nearly prefect PSAT scores, in his own mind, the next Ben Casey.

"Medical schools do make a few appointments to top graduates for research," Daily explained. "But most of those who complete their training end up in the traditional role of family doctor, a general practice. You should develop a good bedside manner, young man. Don't plan to be the one who finds a cure for polio."

Little was foreseen in those days of the changes technology were to bring to the practice of medicine—the diagnostic instruments, computers, and sophisticated chemical analyses that would shift the center of attention from talking with people to analyzing printouts. Patty recalled a picture in her physics textbook of Madame Currie, examining the bones of her own hand in a primitive X-ray. She couldn't remember if Madame Currie had been a medical doctor or a scientist. What, by the way, was her first name?

"What do you have, Patricia?" Ray asked, laying his condom on the fountain's rim. He might have wanted to hide his confusion at her apparent familiarity with his surprise.

"Actually, it's 'Patience,' not 'Patricia.'"

"Patience? . . . Oh . . . sorry."

"But I prefer 'Patty.'"

"Ah. Patty."

Out of her pocket Patty then took a rectangular plastic case, perhaps three inches wide by five inches long, only a quarter of an inch thick. She pried the top up to reveal a grid, five rows of seven circles, 35 little caps. Popping up one tiny lid, she pulled a single small pill, about half as large as an aspirin, out of a slight recess. She held the white dot up between thumb and forefinger, smiling. It stood out before them even in the dim light.

"What is this?"

"It's a birth control pill."

"What . . . ?"

"You take it, silly, to keep from getting pregnant."

"I . . . ?"

"Not you. A girl. A woman. Not me, of course. I'm Catholic."

"But what good is it tonight? For me?"

"This is just to show you something you didn't know about."

Now Patty was angry. What had he been thinking, after all? And she had gone to some trouble to bring this item for display! Show and Tell did not mean Show and Use.

The case was a dummy set, shown her by one of the nurses at the medical school. Mary Joyner had assisted the head of obstetrics in his presentation. But Patty had chatted with the R.N. after the session, hearing some remarkable things about medical procedures of the future. And she was given this demonstration kit to take back to her school.

The pills were sugar, of course, but their size illustrated how powerful the genuine medicine would be. Each pill rested in its own capped recess, labeled for the day of the month. The drug companies were taking great pains to make the system simple for the women who would take them.

Patty had been intrigued by how the medication worked, the hormones and responses. But she doubted Ray was interested in a scientific explanation. So she replaced the pill, closed the case, and slipped her surprise back into the sundress pocket. Then she reached out to take up his condom from the fountain's rim.

XV.

The event Ray kept secret for forty years occurred a few blocks from the Saigon villa in which he lived and worked. He was escorting a newbie to a MAC-V office so he could complete a part of his in-country training. But both had paused to enjoy an early morning sight. About a dozen young girls in Áo Dàis were on the other side of Tu Do Street, standing by a fountain before their school day was to begin.

Oblivious of the passing traffic — pedestrians, bicycles, scooters, rickshaws, tiny economical cars, military jeeps, trucks, buses — the girls would lean close to each other, whisper, and giggle. Ray was in awe of their unselfconscious youth, their smiles and laughter

It was still the dry season, and Ray, sufficiently adapted to the climate not to feel the heat, was amused at his overweight comrade's heavy perspiring and shortness of breath. "You'll get used to it," he promised.

Still, out of consideration, he paused to take pictures of the street scene, careful not to point the camera at the girls. He shot a vendor selling bright tropical fish in water-filled plastic bags hung from a bamboo structure on the back of his bike. Scanning up through the sunlight, he saw the leaves of trees, a deep green, above a Western style office building. Storefront planters on the sidewalk featured multicolored blossoms. Fresh fruit and vegetables poked out of baskets balanced at the ends of poles on vendors' shoulders.

"What war?" thought Ray once again. The city was peaceful, prosperous, vibrant. The schoolgirls in white were to be beneficiaries of America's determination to save their country. He slipped the lens cap back on the camera and secured the

113

case and strap. Pickpockets were the most dangerous threat here.

A bus passed between the two soldiers and the girls across the street. The rocket must have landed directly on the other side because the vehicle jumped into the air, then flipped over onto its side. The explosion deafened Ray, though he and PFC Martin were protected from the force of the blast by the bus.

Turning, as training had taught him, to race back to the compound, he realized Martin was frozen in place. He reached out and grabbed him by the elbow. As Ray yanked on the man's arm, he looked just once and saw the bright red spread over white, the sandals and sleeves flung along the sidewalk and into the churning fountain water, the one girl crawling.

XVI.

"I want to see this," Patty said.

"Oh, I can open it. But it ought to be used, if I do."

She suspected this to be a lie, of course. "Well, I do want to see it on."

"On?"

"On."

"Well, OK. Fine. Come on. Let's find a place."

"No. Here."

114

"Here?"

"Here. We're alone. It's dark. Show me."

She took the foil packet, deftly tore off one edge, and returned his surprise to him. Then, rising and putting one knee on the brick wall so that she leaned over him, she kissed him, one hand caressing his cheek, the other resting on his shoulder.

"Mmmm," he said.

"Mmmm-mmmm!" confirmed she.

Measuring these new sensations of kissing, Patty heard a rattling of the package, a fumbling at zipper and clothes. Gee, I guess he can keep on kissing and put this thing on without looking, Patty decided. I bet he can pat his head while rubbing his stomach — or whatever!

Keeping two hands on his shoulders, Patty stood up. Ray seemed at first to want to rise with her, to sustain the kiss. But he must have realized that his pants, the belt loosened and the zipper open, restricted him. So he ended up sitting uncomfortably on the fountain's rim, the pool a dark background to a goofy grin visible in the dim light.

"Oh, oh, oh," he moaned imploringly.

"Hm, hm, hm," Patty responded, admiring his ability to kiss and that part of him newly visible.

Patty never did arrive at a completely satisfactory explanation of what happened next.

115

She considered it first an act of God or destiny. But it might also have been simple chance. Later she thought perhaps some testing of the electrical and hydraulic systems had been under way all along in the lull of the university's summer schedule. She finally decided it might also be one more incidence of her own good timing.

Whatever the cause, at the precise moment Ray leaned back to look up at Patty with a face openly desiring, and when Patty stood looking down at his proud display, the fountain behind him and the lights around them suddenly cut on. There was a rich whoosh of water, a blinding flash of bright, and boy and girl jumped in surprise.

Patty's leap merely put her a few steps away from the fountain's two-foot high brick wall. Ray, hampered by his clothes, lost his balance, tottered, and then fell backward into the fountain's pool. The splash his slender frame made produced a miniature version of the fountain's rising structure of red, blue, and yellow shapes.

Patty turned in time to see the column of water spread, peak, and return to the surface. Putting her hands comfortably back in the pockets of her summer sundress, Patty smiled at the display. The Show Me Institute was turning out to be just what she had hoped!

XVII.

"There's been a shooting at Virginia Tech, dozens of victims," Ray told Patty on the phone, his voice weak. She realized immediately that it was the same April date on which he had witnessed the slaughter on Tu Do Street. "We're locking everything down on campus. I don't know when I'll be home."

"Do you want me to come over? I could help at the Health Center, counseling or just being there."

"No. No. You just stay home, or go to St. Theresa's. There's an organization in place here. But I'll call again if I need you."

Watching the news over the next few days, Patty was reminded of the University of Texas tower shooting, when a man killed more than a dozen and wounded something like thirty people. It had happened only a few years before Ray went to Vietnam.

Three were killed and eleven wounded at a New York high school in the next decade. The 1980s saw a woman at Washington State University kill two boys and then herself. The Columbine massacre seemed to convince the nation that schools were no longer ivory towers, safe from deadly assault. Virginia Tech was not an anomaly.

She also knew that women trying to go to school in Afghanistan had been hung in public squares and stoned to death. How long would the presence of U.S. troops be necessary there to make education available to all who sought it? Had we stayed in Vietnam long enough or too long?

She and Ray had grown up in something that—in retrospect and in memory—resembled paradise. But, of course, it had never been the Eden they believed in as teenagers. An earnest Victorian society simply worked very hard to keep the most dehumanizing acts of violence out of the public's awareness—perpetrators behind bars and stories sanitized.

Since the 1960s, future baby-boomers had experienced an ongoing education in the depravity of humankind. "Show me," they had asked innocently as children; and history did so with a vengeance. Still, they also continued to learn about the steady efforts of ordinary citizens—educators among them—to reduce or contain violence in American society.

Ray's retirement, Patty concluded, would be a retreat, but not a complete one, any more than the summer institute, graduate school, careers, or family had been. The world's narrative had many threads, and their responsibility was to weave their parts into the whole as well as they could.

On the morning he was to give his retirement remarks to the university community—only a week after the massacre in Blacksburg—she offered Ray her view, beginning with his fall into the fountain. That evening, after a dinner and a

118

bit of roasting, he told a sobering but a forward-looking tale to his colleagues and well-wishers.

Jody

Standing at the grave outside La Mancha, New Mexico, Chris asked, "How the hell did this happen?" On the headstone, he read the name, unconnected to any group.

All Malcolm said in response was, "Jody," and Chris understood . . . or thought he did.

Jody was the mythical boy back home who made time with a GI's girl when he was overseas. The three men had served together in Vietnam, and all had yearned for girls back home at the same time their jealousy conjured up different men in bed with them.

"But he married the girl of his dreams," insisted Chris "He got, in fact, 'The Girl Down the Block.' So, what happened? Did Jody just hang around for ten years, then move in on her?"

Malcolm sighed. "He . . . did, but it's not quite what you think. Let's go somewhere and get a beer. I'll explain."

Chris read it again: "Bud Anderson. 1945-1975." No indication of family, profession, accomplishment, religion. "Not even an R.I.P.," he sighed and went with Mac.

On the way to find a place to talk, Chris remembered some of the 'Jody calls,' marching chants common to Army training as far back at least as World War II. The leader sings each line, and the company echoes: "I don't know, but I've been told, [*I don't know, but I've been told,*] Jody's charms are good as gold. [*Jody's charms are good as gold.*]" They all join in on the refrain: "Give me your left, [step, step], your left [step, step]. Give me your left, your left, your left."

The verses are sometimes improvisational and, with a good storyteller, can go on as long as the march does. With every step and every verse, Jody takes over the girl's life, the G.I.'s former world. "Send your money home to mom," they sing to each other. "You ain't goin' to the prom."

Like many such chants used to coordinate new recruits, the Jody songs stressed a future life with comrades that would replace the civilian past, their new identity as soldiers. The trio of former graduate students had laughed at the prospect, convinced that their Army experience would not change them in the least. When their two years were up, the gap in their student careers would be closed, healed, invisible.

As they waited for two Dos Equis in a downtown cafe, Mac asked, "When did you last see Bud? He changed more than you probably realize."

"It's maybe three or four years, I guess. I went to a conference at DC, filling in at the last minute for a colleague, and I thought it would be neat to just drop in on Bud at the VA. They don't do anything in Washington, of course, so . . . ."

He knew anti-government remarks would be well received by Mac, though he himself had been surprised more than once to find the stereotype inaccurate. The same thing had happened to him with organized religion. He was still surprised to find himself become a committed Lutheran.

"Bud started out there as energetically as he did graduate school," admitted Mac. They had all begun an American Studies Ph.D. program at Vanderbilt in 1967, before student deferments were eliminated. "But the situation didn't turn out as advertised. Abandon hope all ye who enter the labyrinth of bureaucracy."

Chris scanned the low room of El Descanso del Vajero. There was a counter along one wall with perhaps twenty stools, a dozen Formica topped booths, an old time juke box in one corner (though Western music was piped in from somewhere else). Their Anglo presence didn't quite fit this scene.

Little of their weekend, now that he thought about it, was turning out as he had predicted when he called Mac, proposing a pilgrimage to La Mancha from their homes back east. They had not foreseen the effects of hard times in the oil industry on their friend's hometown, the working class culture of his family, the bleak, landscape of southern New Mexico. It was as if hot dry winds had blown away most living things.

Mac went on. "Bud wasn't as eager about graduate school after 'Nam either, though he was one of the few who finished exactly on the four-year schedule we were all supposed to follow—

with, of course, the two-year hiatus. On the surface, he fulfilled the model for the perfect doctoral student."

Chris thought back. "I guess he was having trouble with drinking even then, though. I'd hoped that ended when he married Lou."

He recalled one late-night call. At the time, he convinced himself it was an anomaly. "Can you give me a ride?" Bud had asked. This was after they had returned to Vanderbilt, before any moved away to permanent jobs, and when Bud was just starting to date Lou.

"Sure," Chris told Bud, assuming he'd had car trouble. "Where are you? I can be there is no time." Both Chris' wife and infant daughter were already asleep. He was trying to complete a chapter of his dissertation.

"I'll need you to . . . um, sign for me. That okay?"

"Sign?"

"The bail. I've guaranteed the money, but there has to be a co-signature."

Bud had been stopped for drunk driving, was sober enough to go home, but not to drive. He'd also had to post bond. Chris had never thought he'd be picking up a good friend from jail. The only scenario he could imagine that would land Bud in 'the joint' had to involve being dumped by Lou, but he never asked for details and never learned any.

Louise Kelly was a Nashville television star who played the host of a daily morning kids show, "The Girl Down the Block." An idealized version of your best friend's older sister— whether you were a boy or a girl—she told stories, sang songs, and did craft projects with school children from the audience. Bud had fallen in love with her television personality before he went overseas and dreamed of coming back to woo her.

Mac noted. "He certainly drank over there."

The three had had many nights of indulgence, though no one thought of them then as "binges." That was a phenomenon the next generation of college students brought before the public to the point that a new term had to be coined to identify it.

"If you were in the Army, of course you drank . . . and drank . . . and drank." admitted Chris. "I went without beer for a year when I got out, just to be safe. And I still won't drink the hard stuff. I could see I had too much of a taste for it; it could ruin my life."

"Well, that's not really what ruined Bud's," Mac said.

"Right. Jody. Who was Jody and how did he get to Lou?"

"You guys want another?" asked their waitress, "Izel" according to the stitching on her outfit. Chris realized she was both young and attractive. He wondered if she was old enough to be serving alcohol, or if anyone here would care. When he and his wife went out to eat, it was with the kids to one of the chain family restaurants; so this was different from his routine. It might be called something like down-home Western country eating.

"Sure," said Mac to Izel about another round. Chris, looking about, seemed to think the end-of-the-workday crowd was keeping an eye them. Did they suspect these gringos of checking out the local girls? Maybe the two, in sports jackets and ties, looked like undercover agents from the immigration service, ready to report illegal aliens. (He always wore formal wear to travel, believing the look earned him better treatment on airlines and at restaurants.)

"Jody comes a bit later," explained Mac. "Remember how Bud extended?"

Chris knew their friend had signed on for another tour in Vietnam to earn an early release from his three-year commitment. It also got him an extra R & R (Bangkok) and money to travel when he was out.

"Right. It made no sense to me, though he always said being a Personnel Specialist at Cam Rahn Bay was safer than trying to walk across the street in downtown Albuquerque."

"Well, that extra time did give him enough money to spend several months in Europe, hitchhiking from youth hostel to youth hostel. It's how he met The Girl Down the Block."

"I'd forgotten that. It was somewhere in the south of France, right?" He sipped his beer, wondering how many he would drink and if he shouldn't put something in his stomach before he had too many.

He and Mac had met at the Albuquerque airport in the middle of the day and driven straight down to La Mancha. He'd thought the airport for such a well known city would be huge, but it resembled terminals he'd flown out of in Huntsville and Montgomery. Used to conventional institutional decor, though, he was surprised by the turquoise and silver decorations, the landscape murals done in a Georgia O'Keefe style, the old Route 66 memorabilia displayed in an unaffected manner.

"Bud actually sent me a postcard with his news. Something like: 'Picked Up my Pin-up on the Riviera. Eat your heart out.'"

"He must have swept her off her feet, having idealized her for more than three years. He was some romantic and could lay on the talk!"

Mac pulled the plastic-covered menu from behind the sugar dispenser. "I'd better have something to eat." He winked. "Just hope we don't get Montezuma's revenge from whatever they put in their enchiladas!"

Chris chuckled, but softly, again scanning the locals. More were coming in—dusty, tired looking, Spanish speaking. He and Mac had planned to spend the night at the closest motel, which was outside Las Cruces, meet again with the Andersons, and then fly home from Albuquerque the next day. Maybe they should drive back to the airport tonight.

"Courtship was short and sweet, as you remember: elopement and delayed announcement." Mac chuckled. "Know what Bud told me sealed the deal about her?"

"No. All that happened pretty fast, and I was busy with my own mess—dissertation, fatherhood, job search. It was not going the way I thought it would."

When they had all started graduate school, universities across the country were expanding, new positions were being created, the future looked bright. They watched their colleagues who were finishing choose between high-powered research positions (at, say, New York-Buffalo) or spectacular places to live (Hawaii).

Most of his class ended up taking two or three years out for military service, however; and President Nixon, apparently resenting the academic world, slashed federal funding for higher education in his first term. So job prospects by 1973 or '74 were bleak. Chris's getting an appointment at Troy University at Ft. Rucker,

Alabama, was considered successful placement under the changed circumstances.

"Well," explained Mac, "Bud told me about Lou and her television identity as the Girl Down the Block. That was what the public saw, the kids and their parents. During the filming it was another story. She was a bit of a flirt, and the cameramen, all young, tried at every session to shoot up her dress. The station wouldn't let her wear slacks, and skirts were short in those days."

"That turned Bud on?"

"It turned me on!" laughed Mac. "'The True Behind-the-Scenes Story of Children's Television,' or 'The True and Lovely Behind on the Girl Down the Block.'"

"I'm sure she had other good qualities." The few times he had been with Lou, she'd seemed as sweet and innocent as her on-air personality. He knew, though, to factor's Mac's reports through the prism of appetite.

"Anyway, what we never thought about was what was going on during his second tour in Vietnam."

"That changed Bud?"

"It did, or it brought out a Bud that had always been there."

Chris thought about his own return from Southeast Asia after one tour. It was nothing like the newsreel images from the end of World War

II: the iconic families on New York City docks, the girl bent backward in an ensign's kiss, the Main Street parades. At least his girl was waiting, no Jody in that story:

Saw my girl in a dream last night.

Man, it gave me quite a fright.

Sound Off. [*One, Two*] Sound Off. [*Three, Four.*]

Saw her belly was starting to swell,

Jody's the daddy, sure as hell.

Sound Off. [One, Two, Three Four.]

Amanda had put her arms around him, took him to her bed, said they would meet the world on their own time. Their daughter was born three years later.

Mac came back at the same time, but would not marry for more than a decade after his return, had divorced twice, and was again single. Bud was delayed that extra year. The three saw each other less and less as they went their separate ways, eventually to Oregon, Alabama, and the nation's capital.

"So," Chris asked, studying the steaming burritos, rice, and refried beans on the kind of plate he'd handled as a busboy at his hometown hotel twenty years earlier. "So, what about that extra year . . . Well, I guess it turned out even less than the standard twelve months, didn't it?"

Mac was digging into his food and gesturing for another beer. "Right. Nixon was giving drops to get the troop numbers down and convince the country he was ending the war. Ending the war, my ass!"

As he said that, he studied the form of Izel, now rushing past with customers at every table. "Speaking of ass . . . she's got a sweet one."

"Whoo! Hot" cried Chris and reached for his beer. "Not her," he whispered. "The beans. I thought I knew spicy food!"

"Tex-Mex can be more Mex than Tex, good buddy."

Chris took another long drink. "Okay, so that extra year. Bud never told me it was any different from his first: 'More of same-same . . . and more and more and more,' he said."

"You know, they had a daughter?"

"Bud and Lou?"

"Right. And Lou wanted another child. She was going to give him a son, the complete American family unit, you understood."

Chris understood more than he would say. It was what he had wanted unconsciously more than he'd known.

One night a few years earlier, the rest of his family asleep, he was watching television. Cable had begun to show reruns, in non-prime time hours, of the family sitcoms of the late 1950s and early '60s — *Father Knows Best, Leave it to Beaver, The Dick Van Dyke Show*. In one instance Chris was shocked to encounter what seemed a perfect depiction of himself, of his pre- and post-military life.

The black-and-white show caught his attention from the beginning with an aerial view of a typical middle-class small town or suburb. It could have been, Chris thought at first, the western edge of Fairfield, the town along Missouri Route 66 where he had been born and raised. Several church steeples rose up through the trees, and he could see glimpses of larger buildings likely to be banks, civic buildings, businesses.

The camera zoomed down to the rooftops of a neighborhood with conventional two-bedroom brick, clapboard, and stone-faced homes along tree-lined streets. Rock walkways led from cement sidewalks to front porches, and tidy yards featured modest flower beds, attractive shrubs.

When the camera settled at ground level and panned to one side, Chris could see a smiling woman with two children and a dog come out of one house's front door. They looked from the stoop up the street to see a man in a suit, briefcase in one hand, striding toward them. He, too, was smiling. It was the archetypal American middle-class (white) family, each person assigned and satisfied with a role.

What struck Chris that night was how much the father resembled him, the wife his wife, the house the very home where he now lived in a small town in the South. He even felt he could smell Amanda's signature baked chicken dish steaming in the kitchen, hear National Public Radio playing from the den, taste cold dark beer in a frosted glass. How could it be that he and his family were featured in a television show three decades before they existed?

Was it possible, he thought, that, as he was growing up, he had internalized this stereotypical pattern of family life from the world of television and then unconsciously reproduced it by going to college, falling in love, building a career, obtaining mortgage, car, and bank accounts?

He'd always believed he was a rational planner, the architect of his own future. He consistently analyzed choices at every turning point, made decisions only after constructing detailed lists of pros and cons, pursued a valid course among options that he had determined. Surely, he hadn't followed some path drawn by social structures created in the past and embedded in his mind the way a mother hen's identity is imprinted on a chick's heart?

Still, if he had been shaped by culture, there was nothing in his experience that led to or departed from La Mancha.

True, all those WWII movies he'd watched as a boy at the UpTowne gave him models for himself as soldier, though his war had seemed to have more of an antecedent in the Korean conflict than the European or Pacific theater of his father's era. Service in the rear had been different only in that rockets might land on you, but not bombs.

Oddly, nothing he'd imagined beforehand included the loss of a good friend after the fighting was concluded. His thoughts selfishly concerned his own survival, the potential sorrow brought to his family, a remote possibility of crippling injury, months-long recovery, or even invalidism. Never the fact of Bud Anderson's death years after the war.

"Let's have one more round," he said to Mac, who was already gesturing again to Izel. "I think Lou might have been expecting the last time I saw Bud. If she wanted another child, where did Jody fit in? And who was Jody?"

"This is a bit convoluted, I'll have to admit, but he was at Cam Rahn Bay with Bud after we were gone. He was an officer in the old outfit."

"And Bud got along with him? Ah, I see now. After they were both back stateside, he and Bud got together somewhere, and he said 'Want you to meet my wife'; they all went out. So, it's not the usual Jody back home while you're way, but a Jody nonetheless."

Mac gave him an odd smile. "Still not quite there, buddy, though there is a reversal of the usual in this triangle scenario." He looked away, but not really at anything in El Descanso del Vajero.

In his mind Chris heard another Jody chant:

I don't know but it's been said.

Jody's sleepin' in your bed.

Am I right or wrong? [*You're right!*]

Don't look back cause Jody's there,

But where you're goin' you won't care.

Am I right or am I wrong? [*You're right!*]

He had learned to numb his desire at Cam Rahn Bay, but he also knew there were plenty of ways to release that sexual energy even then. This Jody must have respected no limits.

"You see," Mac continued. "Bud and this Jody were good friends in 'Nam. I mean . . . really . . . close."

Chris studied Mac's face. Then he asked. "Are you saying they were too close? Bud wasn't gay!"

"Well, that's what he finally confessed to me. He called me about a year ago. Said he was in love, his marriage was over, he was heading for Texas with someone else."

"And that someone was a guy?"

"He was. Said his name was Jack. Jack had gotten out of the Army and started his own business, recruiting for employers, quite successful, wanted Bud aboard professionally and personally. They were buying a house together in Austin and were going to renovate it as their dream home."

"Whew! That's a lot for me to take in." The dinner crowd around them had thinned, but the same group of men at the counter still seemed to be keeping an eye on him and Mac. Most were about his own age, but definitely from a different socio-economic group. "Look, let's get out of here. Hell, let's drive back to Albuquerque tonight. Find a motel and catch our flights tomorrow."

Mac shrugged. "All the same to me, though . . . ." He eyed Izel one more time as he leaned over to wipe off a table. "Hate to leave without appreciating the local attractions."

"Truth be told, I don't think the Andersons really meant it when they said to come by again."

Chris had written to the family after he heard that Bud had taken his life. Mac wasn't sure where he was buried, as Lou had broken off all communication with him about eighteen months previously. Chris didn't ask Mac the cause of that estrangement, though he believed Mac and Bud liked to party together, perhaps too much for someone married to a woman with her own profession, a young mother.

But now it was beginning to make sense, sadly. Lou's world must have collapsed after the storybook romance, the two careers in the nation's capital (she'd returned to television as an exercise guru), the growing family. She probably saw all of her husband's old friends as people who should have told her the truth . . . or even as possible former lovers.

The Andersons responded to Chris's letter with a copy of a painfully terse obituary from the local paper: dates, surviving family members, private service, interment at (the oddly named for the region) Evergreen Cemetery. No cause of death.

When they arrived at the small adobe house on the edge of town to express their condolences and ask for directions to the gravesite, the parents acted as if they spoke little English. In a patriotic region that produced many volunteers for the military, it didn't make sense that they seemed displeased when he reminded them that they had been fellow soldiers with their son. Now he felt he was beginning to understand why.

Bud had been the baby of the family, considerably younger than his three sisters, who all lived away from La Mancha. His outstanding schoolwork earned him a full scholarship to Baylor, and at Vanderbilt he seldom spoke of his family. When he did, however, Chris felt he showed great affection for them and almost regretted the distance his education had taken him from their way of life.

"We can send the Andersons a note from the airport, say we had to get back. Hell, I don't think they need any more stress." He took up the check. "Let me get this. You okay to drive?"

"Sure. I'll make that one stop, get a cup of coffee to go."

As Chris stood at the register, two men from the counter came over. "You not from here, are you?" one said.

"No, no, just came down . . . to pay a visit to the cemetery." He looked nervously at this man, short, heavily built, deeply tanned. Over this shoulder Chris saw that his friends were watching them, perhaps able to hear their conversation.

Scenes from Spaghetti Westerns that had been playing in the back of his mind since they walked in the diner began to flash before his eyes. Clint Eastwood, the man without a name, arriving at a nearly deserted town attacked by brutal members of some outlaw gang. You knew, because it was a movie, they'd pay in the end.

"Family?"

"Ah, no, old friend. Old Army buddy, in fact."

There was a pause. "You in Vietnam?"

"Yes."

Chris didn't know what to expect: being accused of baby killing; told to say away from their women; asked if he wanted to buy a little weed from over the border. He was in unfamiliar territory, to be sure.

"So, maybe a friend of Bud Anderson, huh?"

Mac had come up to the group by now, his eyebrows raised in a question. Chris gestured to him. "Yeah, we both are. He was in our unit, but we also knew each other . . . at school." He decided it wasn't necessary to say "Vanderbilt."

The group's apparent leader looked back to his friends at the bar, waved them over. Then he turned to the two visitors. "Our amigo, Bud. We're going to miss him. It's good you've come down here. Thanks, man." He shook Chris's hand, then Mac's. The others did the same.

The locals stood for a minute looking at Chris and Mac. Then the leader said, "Look to yourself, my friends. It's a shitty world out there sometimes."

On the drive back, Mac finished the story, at least as far as he knew it.

"I think it was pills. He'd started adding them when the drink wouldn't take him far enough."

"But wasn't he with Jack, wasn't he happy in Austin?"

"At first, sure, but, near as I can tell, Jack remained the officer and Bud the enlisted man in that little army. Bud couldn't come up to standards."

Chris knew all relationships involved power and expectations. It was a miracle when what you were matched the needs of your partner in a conventional or unconventional union.

"So, let me get this straight. Bud left his wife and child—with maybe a son on the way—followed this guy to Texas, then got dumped."

"That's how I see it." Mac drove on through the darkness in silence. Both were lost in thought.

Chris looked out the window, hoping to see stars. All he'd read about New Mexico stressed the beauty of the night sky. How could he spend one night in the Land of Enchantment and have clouds obscure its most famous natural feature?

"I wish I'd known what was happening to Bud," he lamented. "You get so busy with life, you know; you lose touch. I was still picturing him in Washington, rising through government ranks at the Veterans Administration, a prosperous and productive career. What did I know?"

"I did worry at one time," Mac said slowly. "I worried that . . . maybe something I'd shown Bud . . . that I'd contributed to his death. But I'm pretty sure it didn't. At least, I hope it didn't."

Chris wasn't sure he wanted to hear this. Mac had been known in graduate school for always having access to drugs. It was mostly pot, but he also experimented with more potent stuff. Some said he got hooked on crack for a time.

"Go on."

"Well, you weren't ever part of it, I know, but some of us back in Nashville, we did some experimenting with drugs and . . . some kinky sex stuff. And when I saw Bud that last time, I told him some of things you could do . . . with a bit of assistance. But you had to be careful. If you go too far . . . well, you won't come back."

"Jesus."

"I gave it all up myself, too damn scary. And I don't think . . . I'm sure Bud never went there. And Jack," he chuckled, "though queer, was straight in some ways."

Chris didn't want to learn any more, sorrowing at the blasted faces of Bud's parents, the decent men who'd lost a comrade, the Girl Down the Block's undeserved pain. Regret would haunt him the rest of days as surely as the bleak tombstone, the windblown cemetery, the depressed town.

"Not even an R.I.P.," he muttered and turned his head to the window. "Save me, Jesus, from my sins."

~~~

Re-up

"You're going to what?" I was incredulous.

"I think you heard me, Sandra," he replied in that irritatingly flat voice he can use—as if he were talking to one of his staff.

I knew immediately I'd regret the words that came to my lips. But the frustration of the previous weeks must have been too much, and out they came: "I suppose next you're going to have your foreskin restored."

He was as stunned at my coarseness as at the (completely unfair) insult, pausing just a moment before turning to walk toward the basement stairs, where he could practice his three-rail billiards. Much later, he would tell me the retort on the tip of his tongue. It also involved a surgical procedure, requested by some older women—or by their husbands. Generously, he did not utter it.

Even if he imagined that mean comeback, the hurt on his face haunts me still. But I felt at the time any act to stop his madness would be justified.

He was in his sixth decade on the planet, and what possible role he could play in the War on Terror was a mystery to me. Given his recent irritability about work, occasional insomnia, the vacant look in his eyes, I felt this crisis was more psychological than a genuine desire to be a player in world affairs. But that didn't mean I had an answer to his condition; and his behavior was reminding me more and more of the most difficult period of our relationship.

I didn't start snooping on him at the first signs of restlessness (as I had long ago), but I did begin again to catalog in my mind the unexpected changes in his behavior. What he was saying and doing recalled the way he had been during that first year back from Vietnam, before we were married. Then, I had secretly taken notes for the counseling sessions he finally agreed were necessary.

I was okay with the resumption of his competitive billiards career, even if it was a first sign of his dissatisfaction with the status quo. Men in their fifties often find new or revive old interests, especially once the children leave home. And with inevitable physical decline, success at a sport can reinvigorate the whole person.

Ever since 9/11, Arthur had become much more unpredictable—at times lethargic, at times manic—and perhaps depressed (though not, I hoped once more, clinically so). It never occurred to me that he could want to be go to war a second time.

"Mid-life crisis," our daughter said when she was home for Christmas. Jennie was in her second year at South Central Missouri State University down in Fairfield. A psychology major, she possessed the same innocence and belief in neat diagnostic categories I'd had at her age.

However, after he went into a deep sulk just because I was late coming home from work, she did ask, "He's okay, though, right?"

She and I were having coffee after a dinner at which our leading questions and his short responses had led nowhere. "Funny you should wonder," I replied. "He does seem to be brooding now and then. He gets up to read a lot, after he thinks I'm asleep."

"Read what?"

"Well, *The Lord of the Rings*, most recently. He says he devoured the books in college, but this time it's different. He finds them more relevant to the current global situation. And he wonders how the movie trilogy will add to the legend."

She and her brother were of the Stars Wars generation and didn't know Tolkien's work, even though the movie series owed much to earlier books. Just as Alex Guinness had had many great roles before he became Obi Wan Kenobi, so Lucas' multi-generational wars between the Empire and rebels echoed the three-book tale of the ring.

"Hmm. Keep an eye on him, Mom. You don't want Daddy acting like the twenty-something version of himself, suddenly buying a red Mazda Miata, and looking for a girlfriend."

Actually, I felt I could deal with that sort of conventional problem. We had shared so much that I believed a fling unlikely at best, short term at worst. I worried that this was something else, something deeper, older, and more difficult to resolve.

So, as I say, I started searching for the true causes of his mood swings, even the possibility of a mild, retroactive, delayed post traumatic stress reaction (if there is such a thing). While I didn't know exactly what he'd done (or witnessed) in Vietnam, I knew it had shaken him. And that's why I was thumbing through his mail before I laid it, as usual, on the little table by the door. There I found the material.

"This came for you," I handed him the packet of papers from — of all places, to my mind — the United States Army. "Going back to school?"

Since he'd never used all of his GI Bill benefits, I figured this was really about programs for veterans. Having been drafted right after graduation from Westminster College in Fulton with an economics major, he'd ended up in military intelligence. He had six months stateside at Fort Hood before his assignment in Southeast Asia.

"Considering it," he answered and took the large envelop into the den. He'd been playing billiards at the Y this Saturday morning, where a league had recently been created. He was in the next-to-last stage of a round robin tournament.

I followed him. "Public policy, then?"

"Something like that."

144

It was clear he wasn't going to give details. Promoted the previous year to head of data analysis at the state Division of Accounting, though, it would be an odd time to make a career change. I certainly didn't want to leave Jefferson City, where we'd grown up and returned to raise our family.

"You watching basketball this afternoon?" I asked, more to keep him engaged than to plan the day. "Otherwise, there's a special on cross stitch I might want to look at."

"Pre-season was last week, so, yes, first game's today." He added, but without conviction, "It could be a good year."

He'd been a Hawks fan since he was a boy and the team was in St. Louis, the Cliff Hagan/Bob Pettit years. Each season he believed they would return to the top ranks of the NBA. I felt following the stats gave him a sense of continuity, a feeling of trajectory season by season even when other aspects of life were less connected.

"I assume you renewed your cable subscription for all the games?"

"Um-hm." He clicked on the television and settled into his favorite chair. I noticed that he tucked the package between his hip and the arm of the chair.

I went off to the living room, where I kept my knitting. This was a hobby I had neglected during the years our children were young but recently found relaxing and rewarding. At the same time, a friend at church had enrolled me in a peace shawl project, giving me a renewed sense of connection to people around the globe. Since George W. was busy waging a sequel to his daddy's war, it seemed the world would need all the healing gestures we could make. A group of us met weekly at the parish house to talk politics, study patterns, and pray.

Arthur was not, of course, interested in knitting, but another of his recent fields of interest was religion. And that had led him to be again a regular participant at St. Johns, the church we'd been married in but fell away from for more than a decade. September 11 awakened dormant concerns in Art about the meaning of it all. And recently he'd been engaging our rector in philosophical and theological debate concerning the concept of "a just war." To me—more liberal politically than he—that term just seemed an oxymoron

Our entry into the empty-nest period of adulthood was accentuating such divisions between us rather than (as I'd hoped) rekindling the romantic enthusiasm we had shared when we were first married and before I went back to finish college. I'd taken ten years out when the children were little; and, because some of the courses I had taken earlier were out of date, I needed several extra terms to finish the R.N.

After another decade of part-time work while Ted and Jennie were still in school, I was able to become a full-time nurse and still manage time for the two us to do things together. Rather than the dinner theaters, art shows, or excursions to nearby historic sites we'd often anticipated for this stage of life, however, Arthur spent his time reading, following professional basketball, or whacking the white ball with the red dot into the red ball and the other white ball.

The game he loved was three-rail-billiards. Each player scores when he (or she) hits a ball into another ball, off three cushions, and into the third ball. First player to fifty is the winner. At home in the basement he played imaginary opponents, keeping track of the score by sliding little wooden beads down wires strung above the table. Every fifth bead was blue, every tenth red, all the others the color of the wood.

He had put up other 100-bead wires to keep track of wins and losses against specific fictional players, some modeled on famous ones from real life and others the boys he'd battled in his teen years. He would play matches late into the night, resume them the next day or when he had time. I have no idea how many hours were represented by those beads.

Now, he was good, I'll give you that. And there were only a few at the Y who were genuine matches for him. But I felt there was more to his intensity and that it was putting distance between us.

147

"How about I be your opponent some of the time," I'd offered. "I was pretty good, as you remember."

It was how we'd met, in fact—a mixer at the university. His sister made him come during his thirty-day leave before shipping out to Vietnam. She was trying to keep him busy, and I was taking a break from the busy pre-nursing program.

"Arthur says he can beat any girl here shooting behind his back," Sally told me. "And I'm betting a dollar you'll make him regret his bragging."

"We both have to have the cue behind us to make our shots?" I asked, picking up a cue and trying awkwardly to pass it around my waist in the back.

"No, no," he explained. "You play the regular way. I'll take the handicap. I've . . . I've done this quite a bit." He held the cue with one hand as if it were a drill major's baton, then manipulated the balls with the other like a juggler.

Sally had already told me he had been a state juniors champion and, had there been a respectable professional circuit then, he might have pursued a career. Instead, he'd followed the family's tradition and studied accounting. (Our son Teddy became a CPA; and he, too, is an excellent billiards player.)

Sally was a good friend, and I knew Arthur was headed overseas; so I was ready to be

148

cooperative—to a point. Few of us were enthusiastic about the war in 1968, so we felt for the draftees. Those who enlisted were suspect in some circles, but not mine. My dad and three of my uncles had been in World War II. I admired the courage of those who were willing to respond to the call, even if the cause was less clear than I wished it to be.

"That doesn't seem fair," I countered. "Let's say you shoot with the cue in back, and I'll play left-handed. The winner gets to . . . to, um, have the balls."

He arched an eyebrow. "I don't think we can take them with us . . . the billiard balls, that is." I smiled, and the game was on.

Sally knew I was left-handed and the sorority champion. Two months later Art wrote from Nha Trang demanding a rematch. He also said he'd like to continue the conversation about "handedness, cue strokes, and . . . balls."

After a few sessions in the basement more than three decades later, though, it was clear I wasn't returning to form. He played a patient, deliberate game, making every clear shot and, if he left the balls poorly, figuring the best safety. He was always thinking several shots ahead.

His exact intentions for his future in the real world, though, were unclear to me until last week, when I found out he was not at work. I'd called the office ostensibly to remind him it was our turn to go over to the Livermores for dinner;

149

but it was also another move in my ongoing attitude-check program.

"He left after lunch," Betty, his administrative assistant, told me. "A follow-up appointment of some sort, but not work related."

"Oh, that's right," I lied, and not for the first time recently. "I'd forgotten. I'll get him on his cell."

He didn't answer the cell, so I added this incident to my list of worries. And, after our dinner with Fred and Donna, I decided to look for the right moment to ask a few questions.

He had been withdrawn throughout the evening, yet these were old friends we'd been trading dinners and playing bridge with for many years. Rather than taking in and offering updates on our children, work, and local politics, he let me carry the burden of conversation and declined to finish the rubber from our last time together. We went home early.

While we were drinking coffee the next morning, I told him about Betty's not knowing where he had been the day before. "I know you don't have to inform me of your whereabouts every minute of the day, but you've seemed . . . I don't know, out of sorts lately. Is something bothering you? Should I be worried about . . . how you are?"

He held the paper open in front of him, ostensibly keeping up with his favorite long-running comic strips—*Dagwood, Beatle Bailey, Rex Morgan, M.D.* "You don't need to be worried, but I have been considering a professional change. In fact, assuming I pass the physical, I may reenlist in the Army this summer. You might get to be a military wife at last!"

That's when I made the ugly remark about surgically enhancing his manhood. And he walked away.

If I was surprised at his bizarre intention to re-enlist, I was also stunned at the crack about my wanting to be "a military wife at last." At some point on our honeymoon, it's possible I did confess that I wished I could have been more support for him while he was overseas. But I hadn't exactly declared a desire to have a husband in the service.

We had married eighteen months following his return from Vietnam, six months after his counselor felt he had come to terms with his experience there. I had wanted to look back then only to be sure the way forward was clear.

At Niagara Falls he explained, "Oh, you'd just met me; you didn't know me. And . . . I don't think it would have helped to . . . to have someone else back home." His parents were elderly, and the strain of his service on them had been hard.

"I remember what you read while you were over there, how the country was blaming you guys for the atrocities, not like it was in World War II."

"Frankly, we didn't have time to worry about all that. And you wrote me nice letters from time to time."

"I was inspired by my Aunt Sophia. She posted a letter to my uncle every day for three years. And he saved those letters. I wanted to follow in that tradition."

Aunt Sophia was also my knitting mentor. During the war she'd done the customary making of socks, mittens, scarfs. Later, she would take commissions for special items, sweaters and hats that you couldn't buy in stores. I had inherited her knitting material and the file of patterns, which I had rescued from the attic and begun using not long ago.

When he walked away from me after the foreskin reference, I wasn't about to let the matter go. I followed him down to the basement. "Okay, okay. I may have been a bit hasty there. But, really Arthur, going back into the military now? In middle age? And as unhappy as you were when you were in Vietnam, what would you accomplish?"

"That was then. This is now. Things have changed."

He had taken up his cue and was lagging—rebounding the white ball from the far cushion; the one whose ball is closer to the near bumper takes the first shot. I picked up another cue, bumped him aside with my hip, and lagged with the red-dot ball. "I'll warm you up while you tell me about this. Your decision might affect my life, you know."

He spotted the balls and took his shot, but hastily and without conviction. "It's hard to explain, really. But, ever since we were attacked, I've been wondering what my response should be. A lot of people feel they need to do something."

"I understand that, but join the Army! Didn't you used to sing a song about how dumb it would be to stay in?"

"You remember that? Huh!" He punctuated his statement with a double-corner score. I put the handle of my cue on the floor, folded my hands around the tip, and waited. He could go on a run.

"I remember something about wanting to vomit more than re-up."

"Ah, yes, Well, actually it's 'throw up.'"

"Sing it."

For some reason, it made him smile. While still shooting, he sang to the tune of "The Colonel Bogey March" (which, in the film *The Bridge over the River Kwai*, is whistled by captured British soldiers): "Re-up, and buy a brand new car. Re-up, show what a fool you are. Re-up, I'd rather throw up, than be a lifer, a loser, a dud."

I laughed, but hearing the song was painful. He'd sung it with such anger thirty years earlier. "But now you want to be a lifer?"

He missed his shot and, uncharacteristically, left me with an easy opportunity. "It's funny, I admit. When I was in the Army, I did what I was told, little more. But I was never applying myself with conviction, not as if I believed in it."

"Who could in those circumstances? You were following the French in the decline of an imperial, colonial system—death spiral. We needed to reinforce our commitment to self-rule and independence, to our own rejection of the European model."

"That's true, that's true. But I'm still not happy with how I performed my duties. I was just marking off days on a short-timer's calendar, not building on the efforts of my predecessors. All of us left that job undone. Now . . . I don't know . . . now maybe it's time to get the country back on course again."

"And so you're going to be a good soldier at your age?"

"I'm going to try."

I missed my shot, badly. "Arthur, what did you do over there? What do you need to go back and do again?"

This stopped him. I didn't know if it was because there was a past action he wanted to

154

undo/redo or because he hadn't considered such a possibility.

"I just want another try." The pain on his face melted my anger.

I sighed. After all, he was a grown man; we were financially secure; if it would settle some demons, I could adjust my career again to follow him.

"Listen," he insisted. "It's not as if I'll end up in the infantry. With my data management experience, I could work far from the front, probably without ever leaving the country," He paused. "But I'd give it 100% this time—you know, 'be what I can be.'"

I mulled this over. "Couldn't you do something like this in some other capacity? You don't need to re-enlist to help the nation."

He sighed. "I could, but it wouldn't be the same." He paused. "I've . . . I've always felt a bit of a fraud on Veterans Day. Sure, I was in the Army, served my time, but not the way others did. Certainly not like the WWII vets." He gave a sad chuckle. "It may be silly, I guess, but I want a do-over."

In the next few days I learned that he'd talked with his superiors at the state about a leave of absence and later return to the system, not necessarily to the same position but something similar. He had such a good record and the state recognized the need for a national effort, so they were sympathetic. He gradually convinced me it would not be a break with his past so much as the knitting of different pieces into a larger pattern.

Still, I was hurt that he'd gone this far without even talking to me about his plans. And it hadn't bothered him that this would interrupt yet again my (already) delayed career as a full-time nurse. For many married women my age, this was a time of opportunity, the pursued of dormant if not frustrated ambition. Why not for me?

There was also irony in Art's re-up song, which is why I have always remembered the tune and the alcohol-inspired renditions he and his Army buddies had indulged in from time to time.

Composed on the eve of World War I, "Colonel Bogey" became one of the most popular marches of all time. There are many variations to the lyrics, but during the Second World War, the most familiar line in all versions was "Hitler has only got one ball." In the rest of the verses, other figures in the German high command are said to have other testicular abnormalities. Allied soldiers enthusiastically chanted the song in training — and at bars.

I know this history because of my youthful infatuation with the movie, *The Bridge Over the River Kwai.* "The Colonel Bogey March" raises the morale of soldiers being forced to build a bridge for the Japanese. While Colonel Nicholson (Alex Guinness) is the chief character, I paid more attention to one officer, U.S. Naval Commander

Shears (William Holden), who escapes and, though wounded, reaches a hospital in (what is then) Ceylon.

Actually, this man is not the real Commander Shears, but an enlisted sailor who put on the dying officer's uniform and assumed his rank and privilege. Free from battlefields, he enjoys the attentions of a beautiful (of course!) British nurse, played by Ann Sears. His superior knows the truth about "Shears," however, and "volunteers" him for the suicidal operation to parachute in and blow up the bridge.

I saw the movie when I was very young and had not yet thought about my own education. But the picture of Nurse Phillips caring for the man pretending to be better than he is and fated to die a hero's death stayed with me and became an inspiration for my own nursing career. Now, if Art did re-up, I might become a later day version of this World War Two heroine—proud, but a widow.

Of course, the crisis in our marriage dissolved when Arthur failed the physical. Despite the clerical nature of the role he intended to play, there were minimal criteria he had to meet in order to return to active duty. And high blood pressure created a risk the Army would not accept. Over time we moved on to what I always felt was the underlying issue: his desire to mend a wound in his past.

There were long talks between the two of us. We explored alternatives, even his working for the Army as a civilian. And advice was offered by friends, by Rev. Hightower, by people at work. But, in the end, we slowly came to the conclusion that the roles we had found after his service and my waiting for him were good ones. Our lives had followed courses created by the social system that matched our skills and served the larger good. Rather than attempt to turn back the clock and rewrite history — especially if the avenue he wanted was closed — we realized that we should simply enter into our ongoing lives more fully.

In all this I did keep one matter from Arthur: I might have been able to enlist myself. A good friend at St. Mary's had been an Army nurse in Vietnam, and she was being asked to consider returning in an administrative capacity. It was clear to everyone that medical care for veterans was not adequate. Soldiers, male and female, were suffering more and different injuries than we were prepared to treat.

Beatrice said I could make a contribution as well — assuming I was physically fit, of course. But I knew this would be more than Arthur could bear. Coming to terms with his disappointment was difficult enough already; and for me to take the route he had hoped for would be too much.

So I devoted myself to the same, old-fashioned goals I'd always had: supporting his career and his sense of himself in the world. Fortunately, roles like that of the stay-at-home wife and mom

158

have become more acceptable once again after the most militant phases of women's liberation played themselves out. And it's not as if I'm not using my gifts in a professional capacity. I am, however, a bit embarrassed to admit that, during these months of struggle, I have more than once used a common woman's cheap trick to ease some of Art's pain.

I'm sorry, but men always feel better when they've performed well in bed. And often a woman's pleasure increases simply because his does. In the customary mid-life crisis for men energetic, imaginative lovemaking can be salutary for both husband and wife. And it doesn't have to involve new partners outside the marriage.

After one athletically challenging Sunday afternoon session in the billiard room, for instance, we were recovering, sitting on the floor with our backs to a wall. (In the movies of our youth, we would have been smoking cigarettes.) I asked Arthur if he remembered *Moonraker*, one of the James Bond films from the late 1970s.

"Sure. Well, I remember those movies in general, but they may all have blurred together in my mind. Who was the girl?"

"The woman. But yes, Dr. Holly Goodhead. She and Agent 007 are circling the earth in a space shuttle at the very end of the movie."

"It's vaguely familiar. It's hard not to think of Pussy Galore, whichever movie she was in."

"Ha! That's *Goldfinger*. They're all a lot alike, of course — the women and the plots. But *Moonraker* may be distinctive for producing the series' most memorable line."

One of the billiards cues had rolled to the floor. Without getting up, he stood it against the wall beside him. "Again, I kind of remember," he said.

"After she and Bond have destroyed missiles headed for earth," I explained, "Goodhead asks him to 'take me around the world one more time.'"

He chuckled. "And we know what that means."

"Right. But it's what Operational Command down on earth says that I want you to think about right now." I reached up to the table, took one of the blue chalk cubes, and studied it. Then I said, "Someone — I can't recall exactly who — but someone asks Q what Bond is doing up there. And Q replies, 'I think he's attempting re-entry sir.'"

~~~

The Clean Plate Club

No one was quite sure who founded the group, though most assumed it was Dan. Slowed by a bad back at eighty, he was nonetheless tireless in helping nursing home residents. His wife, who had been permanently changed by a brain fever forty years ago, was a resident; he lived in the connected retirement complex. The idea of the club—to encourage everyone to eat, to stay healthy, maybe even to get well and go home—was endorsed by the family members and friends who were regular visitors, as well as by the staff.

Less frequent guests, like Lester Sole, scoffed at the idea. He told his wife, Penny, "It's like a kids' game. Even if they're in their second childhood, you don't have to act silly yourself." She knew his irritation was caused by something else, though exactly what fracture point in his delicate psyche the club touched upon she had never been able to say—until today.

The nursing home scene depressed Lester in general, though he knew he was abandoning the principles he was instructed to follow in sermons he heard before he arrived: the paths of righteousness. Penny knew he came to Harmony Village with her out of guilt but hoped that would change over time. Neither had connected his anxiety to his time in Vietnam—that one hospital ward, the leg.

"Are you a member of the Clean Plate Club today, Jimmy?" Penny asked as she passed by on the way to the table where her sister Charlotte waited. Jimmy ate at the next table over. Crippled physically by scoliosis and mentally by they didn't know what, he loved attention. Today Jimmy scowled and pointed to a small bowl of stewed tomatoes at his place.

"Goodness!" Penny exclaimed and swooped up the dish. "Someone gave you my tomatoes. You can't have them, Jimmy, and don't you even ask."

She spun on her heel and set them down by Charlotte. Jimmy smiled. Everyone knew he hated tomatoes and would refuse the whole meal if they were at his place. He was also obsessed with the arrangement of his food: vegetables here, bread there, drink and dessert on opposite sites of the plate. A new aide must have made the mistake.

Lester generally came with Penny on Sundays after church. There were enough visitors at that time he could fade into the background and limit his participation in small talk — and, of course, in caregiving. Approaching his sixty-fifth birthday and worried about his expanding waistline, he would eat none of the food he claimed was full of fat. (When Les wasn't there, Dan often remarked that Penny's husband was an *a priori* member of the Clean Plate Club.)

"I didn't see them," whispered Susan Porter, nodding toward the tomatoes. Her mother had her meals at Charlotte's table, and she often helped Jimmy. Mrs. Walker responded to simple questions—such as which items on the printed menu she would like—but not much else. "I'll make sure Daisy knows."

Daisy was the cook, sixty years old, so good at her job and so strong in her opinions that even Mr. Budd would not confront her. She kept order in the kitchen, and in the kitchen staff. They were, in fact, a reliable and remarkable group—underpaid, overworked, yet faithful to the residents. Charlotte, who had had MS for thirty years, was one of their favorites. Mentally sharp, she could only stay in her wheelchair a few hours each day. So, for her, meals were a major social occasion.

"Becky's going to be a member of the Clean Plate Club today," observed Dan, patting his wife's hand. He'd brought her favorite—chicken fingers and French fries—instead of letting them serve the nutritionally balanced meal of stewed tomatoes, mashed potatoes, and country-fried steak. Better that she ate what she wanted now than wake hungry later.

"I can see that," said Penny approvingly. "And are you eating now?" He was allowed one meal a day in the dining hall, but had to fend for himself back at his apartment the other times. Becky's condition was baffling: she was a regular at the bridge table, but couldn't follow the simplest

163

daily regimen. "She can remember who played the four of diamonds four days ago," Dan would explain wistfully, "but can't say what she had for lunch an hour ago."

"Yes, I'm eating. Rachel's already brought the soup," he answered Penny, pointing. "It's good today, but you might not want to ask me what's in it." He pretended to see something odd in a full spoonful. "If it were alphabet soup, it might spell 'mishmash.'"

Regular visitors often helped themselves to items rejected by the residents. The staff looked the other way, as bending the rules assisted the cleaning up, and the food would go into the trash otherwise. An unofficial system complemented institutional policy in this consideration, as it did with the Clean Plate Club.

Lester had pushed a chair up against the outer wall, close enough to their table to take part in conversation if he had to, but set back so that he could at times retreat into his own thoughts.

Sometimes in those thoughts he brooded over this very withdrawal. He had grown up in a close, small family in the '50s, his father a theoretical physicist who kept his distance from everyone at Southwest Missouri State University and in Springfield. Lester had longed to be a part of larger groups, but meaningful community seemed to have eluded him at school, in the Army, at work. Penny, gregarious by nature, and their two outgoing children seemed to constitute the only group in which Lester had a meaningful place. Now and then he even wondered if he would lose that.

Today he was not allowed to remain a wallflower, as Larry Holstein rolled directly over to him and extended a hand. "Good evening, Mr. Sole." Lester shook his hand politely. Silently he wondered exactly what hours of the twenty-four constituted "evening" around here if it was noon right now. In fact, how did you organize sections of a day that involved only eating and sleeping?

One of the newer members of this dinner group, Larry was younger than his tablemates. He had not taken care of his diabetes, though, and lost his legs just below the knee. He was otherwise fit, outgoing, and determined to walk on the new prostheses they were continually adjusting as he went through therapy. "I'm still a whole man," he joked, "so long as the thigh bone's connected to the hip bone."

Because Larry was so lively, Les interacted with him more than with the others. Assuming that black men wanted to talk sports, he'd even made a special effort to watch the NFL playoffs this season. He prepared to exchange thoughts on how lucky the Patriots were to be in a weaker bracket, what formation changes the Bears would have to make in their defense, which Packers had been moved to the injured reserve list.

Mr. Holstein swiveled his wheelchair around to the table. "I see you saved the day," he said to

Penny, gesturing at the bowl of tomatoes. He knew how Jimmy could snap off his glasses, fold them up on the table, and cross his arms across his chest—official posture of rebellion.

"We strive to keep peace," smiled Penny. "Charlotte likes them anyway, so it's a double positive."

Lester recalled meals of his childhood, the fixed places at the dining room table for his parents, him, and his sister. His mother put their food on the plates in the kitchen; you ate what you got, no trading. There was some value in that unchallengeable arrangement, especially compared to the disconnected eating habits of the current world: packaged snacks eaten on the run, order-out pizzas in front of the television, fast food consumed in the car.

He surveyed the other tables in the dining hall, the familiar figures that made him uncomfortable. A woman whose hands were always bandaged— did she eat them if she could? The man with the tic, rhythmically sweeping his thumb across his nose and pausing only when food approached his mouth. (His eyes closed, how did he know?) The woman, small and bent forward, resting her forehead on the edge of the table to block the spoonfuls offered ever so gently. What a pitiful crew here assembled—and for what purpose?

"Did you get your box returned?" Penny asked Dan. He had recently switched service providers, but, because they were in a small town on the edge of the Ozarks, he'd had to package and ship the old receiver to Kansas City. Lester admitted to himself that at least Dan wanted to be connected, bundling Internet, phone, and satellite television to get a lower rate. Retirees were careful to manage their finances, expenses matched exactly to income.

"Betty took it this morning on her way to work."

His daughter Betty, a family counselor, was another Harmony Village regular. Penny claimed Betty was working overtime whenever she visited: arranging bridge games for her mother, helping set up outings to the movies or local concerts for those who could appreciate them, serving as a perennial member of the family advisory board. Lester thought the nursing home administration took advantage of such good will, pretending not to recognize volunteers as workers so they wouldn't show up on the payroll.

Susan asked, "How did the poker game go last night, Larry?" She stood up, ready to take her mother back to her room, but still wanting to show interest in what everyone was doing. When Mrs. Walker stopped eating, she would compulsively stack up whatever was left—as well any extra bowls, utensils, salt and pepper shakers, the plastic flowers within her reach—in an unstable tower. So Susan couldn't linger.

"Well, now, that's a story," Mr. Holstein said, and everyone knew he would take his time telling

167

it. He began with a roll call of the players, though the group was already well known to his audience. He made sure to point out to Les that they were able at the same time to watch the Bears being forced to bring their third-string quarterback off the bench for the last two-minute drill.

Lester saw another batch of residents being wheeled in: the black woman slumped sideways in her wheelchair but alert and insistent on drinking coffee, her torso on a slant barely above the horizontal; the white woman who carried her teddy bear and offered to dance with it, or with anyone; the upright gentleman who smiled broadly at all visitors but had no idea whether one was his daughter or a staff member.

The wheelchair bound, the reclined, the bandaged. They brought up the memory of that ward at the 12th U.S. Air Force Combat Staging Hospital, where the less seriously wounded were recuperating, routine cases like appendicitis were treated, and hypochondriacs fit their symptoms into patterns of chronic disease. Those with horrible injuries and serious illnesses were moved on to Japan and then flown home, if they survived. Les's job that day had been, he felt, insane: to interview the patients for hometown news releases.

Drafted the summer after his graduation from Drury College, he had been trained as a radio reporter by the Army. A network of other educated enlisted men he never knew about had

168

spotted the A.B. on his personnel form as he was being processed in-country. Feeling kinship, they steered his papers to the Army Support Command's information office at Cam Rahn Bay.

There his primary job was to turn standard print releases into broadcast releases, record them on a giant reel-to-reel machine in a studio, and distribute them by established channels throughout the Pacific command. He was grateful for the assignment, as he never left the safety of the giant American base on the coast of the South China Sea.

He tuned back in to the lunch conversation. "On the last hand, Tim was drawing for an inside straight. He'd been on that streak, like I said, one big pot after the other," explained Larry. Susan had reluctantly wheeled her mother out of the dining hall. "Eight, nine, ten, queen. 'You're not getting that jack,' I told him, but would he listen to me?"

"Um, the belly buster," Dan noted. "What were you showing?" He sometimes joined the poker group, but had been playing Clue with his grandchildren last night, thinking about Miss Scarlet, the pipe, the drawing room. His wife, in another room, had bid and made a small slam at the same time.

"I'm showing three fives, so he had to worry about my having four or a full house. But he kept going up, round after round."

"Everybody else out?"

"After the third bet, right. But Billy had a jack and I had one down. So, I knew Tim wasn't getting no jack."

If Les closed his eyes and just listened, he could think Charles still had his legs. They were the same age, and both had been in Vietnam; but Les was pretty sure he'd seen better duty. Race affected assignment, he knew, though education was also a factor. What irony, though, to lose your legs after surviving combat!

"I was fast," Lawrence had told Les one day recently. He'd grown up in a Memphis ghetto but seemed to have lived at one time or another in every major city of the Midwest. Maybe he'd traveled with some semi-pro team in a regional league.

"Speed's an asset in any sport."

"I mean, lightening fast. My mother wouldn't let me play football. On the playground they couldn't catch me; I went through the seams. But I wasn't big, and I knew I could get hurt. So I settled for basketball. I had speed there, too. Didn't matter if it was zone or man-to-man, they couldn't stop me. Played till I was in my forties."

Les and Penny were a regular pair in charity tennis tournaments, she because of the cause, he more the competition. He was careful not to talk about such rigorous physical activity around Larry.

Les remembered that a small group had been playing poker in one corner of the Air Force hospital ward. After identifying the reasons they were there, he asked them questions from the list that had been pre-approved by his C.O.: "How you feeling today?" Getting good treatment?" "Want to say 'hi' to the folks back home?" Answers had been pre-approved as well. Les would edit those that conformed and ship the tape off to a base stateside that had the addresses of radio stations across the country willing to air them. The home office would edit further and produce the individual short interviews.

Les understood that it wasn't a terrible idea, morale building for the troops here and the folks back home. And he was impressed by all the newspapers and radio stations linked together over fifty states and two territories that welcomed such stories. However, he resented one reason Major Tye had sent him: to fill up the monthly report that was supposed to reflect unit efficiency, productivity, mission accomplishment. Really, this mattered in a war zone?

After he'd talked to all who were willing, Les loaded his portable tape recorder and mic, the notepad with attached pencil, and a folder of official forms into a neatly partitioned canvas satchel and headed out the door he thought, wrongly, that he'd come through. Too late, an orderly behind him called out, "Halt!"

Jimmy, finished with his food (a clean plate!), wheeled over to hear the end of Larry's story, though he'd never understood the game. Larry was, as always, patient.

"Well, Jimmy, I won that hand; yes, I did. And a couple more games after that, just like the Chiefs."

Jimmy loved the Chiefs; perhaps a dozen Kansas City caps decorated his chair. He pulled one off the handle and yanked it onto his head. "KansasCityChiefs win beat the Raiders justlikeLawrence he wins the game." Jimmy ran his words together. He also rolled his eyes upward as he spoke, rocking his head left and right as if he were alternately speaker this way and listener that. If others didn't know his favorite topics and the context of the conversation, he could seem to be talking gibberish.

"Look, Jimmy," Dan said, gesturing toward the dining room doors.

Turning his head, Jimmy called out, "MaryBeth." Then, coming back to the table, he told everyone, "It's MaryBeth. MaryBeth" He took pride in announcing visitors.

Mary Beth, who lived in another wing now, came regularly to check on the residents of this dining hall. She was short and tremendously overweight. Her hands and feet were tiny, as if drawn at the end of her limbs by a cartoonist. But she kept on coming, if a bit like a penguin wobbling left and right. She stopped to talk to the friends she'd made when she ate here, asking if

172

they liked the chicken, if they wanted a roll, if they were feeling okay. "Fine," she said to any questions they asked of her.

She had a special greeting for Jimmy, which might have been. "I had the chicken. Pineapple upside down cake was good. You eat the cake?" Mary Beth's speech was nasal and sometimes hard to understand. But she and Jimmy seemed to have decoders for each other, carrying on conversations that no one else could follow.

"Coldtomorrow. Kansas City Chiefs football team Lawrence he wins game."

"Fine."

She patted him on the shoulder and then came over to Charlotte, who said, "Hi, Sugar." Penny's sister called everyone "Sugar," but she knew not just their names, but who their children and grandchildren were, what soap operas they watched, when they had to put off buying groceries until the first of the month because someone was sick and needed medicine.

"Fine," said Mary Beth and examined all the faces at the table.

Lester's mind went back to the ward in Cam Rahn Bay. As he pushed open a door he wasn't supposed to go through, he saw a soldier being carried past on a stretcher. Covered from his chest down with ponchos, he was pleading, "Don't take my leg. Oh, God, please don't take my leg." There was blood all over. Les knew he'd been medevac'd from the field, probably strapped to a chopper's landing skid, enemy fire following the bird across the sky.

Before the orderly could catch up with Les from behind and pull him by the shoulder back through the door, he saw that the man was hugging a leg in his arms. My God! The foot in its combat boot was at the man's head, toe pointed at his ear.

A nurse, holding an IV bottle above the stretcher, looked up at Les's gasp. He saw her fix him sternly with her eyes, lips pressed shut. "Get away," she hissed. "Get away."

Drawing back in horror, he watched the stretcher with its frightful burden disappear through swinging double doors at the end of a hall.

"Rachel. Rachelcoming," announced Jimmy. She was one of his favorite aides, though they all knew Jimmy and catered to him.

"Jimmy, Jimmy, Jimmy," Rachel crooned, coming up to put an arm around his shoulder and lean against his chair. "I heard you had a new girlfriend, Jimmy. What happened? Don't you like me anymore?"

Jimmy laughed loudly, shaking his head back and forth. "Rachel Rachel Rachel. No new girlfriend." All the friends were smiling, even Lester. It was a regular ritual.

174

"I don't know, Jimmy. Carla told me a woman called for you at the desk yesterday. You sure she's not your new girlfriend?"

Most of the kitchen staff were African-American and had worked together for years. Contrary to what the rest of the nation saw in popular representations of small Ozark communities, the population of Harmony was mixed; and economic status more than race created bonds.

Village staff traded tasks on their own, some taking the difficult residents this week, others the next. They brought the food, helped those who couldn't eat by themselves, cleaned the hall afterwards. Management provided regular opportunities for all employees to socialize, and they liked each other. Some hoped over time to get more education and move on to higher paying jobs, still the American dream.

"Oh, no." said Jimmy energetically. "Nonewgirlfriend. Nooneecame to the desk."

"You sure it wasn't Joan, Jimmy? Can you spell 'Joan.'"

Jimmy would practice the names of new residents or visitors. "J-O-A-N," he called slowly. "Joan. No, noJoanhere. NoJoan."

"Okay, Jimmy. I'm going to stay on as your girlfriend then." She tipped back the bill of his Kansas City Chiefs cap and planted a kiss on his forehead. He smiled broadly and readjusted the hat.

"Oh, Jimmy," said Dan. "Rachel's a good friend. Don't you lose her now."

Lester recalled being pulled back from the hallway and escorted through the ward. He felt ashamed, as if he'd violated hospital procedures he should have known about. Out in the open air, he leaned against the Quonset hut's tin wall, struggling to regain his composure in dazzling sunlight and tropical heat.

"Ready to go?" Penny asked Charlotte, handing a glass of tea to Les. "Can you carry this?" He hated it when she drew him into the operation, but took the glass anyway.

Larry reached up to shake his hand again, a ritual Les consistently failed to anticipate. This time, though, he at least had prepared a parting comment. "I'm glad you advised against 'the fool's bet.' Let's hope the odds makers are right about the Jets for next weekend."

As Larry responded, "Amen to that, brother," he also switched his grip on Les' hand, sliding into that complex grasping, twisting, knocking ritual that the grunts used in Vietnam. Les was stunned, but somehow released his muscles from his own control to conform to the rhythm and direction of another veteran. He didn't really know the moves, but Charles' grip carried him along smoothly.

Even as he was swept forward in the dance of fingers, palm, and wrist that would take almost a minute, his mind jumped back to the hospital yard. When he had regained enough composure to start walking away from the compound, the same nurse appeared on the sand path before him. They both stopped, and he heard himself involuntarily asking, "What . . . what happened to that man? How could his leg be . . . where it was?"

Fixing him a second time with a cold stare, she examined his face. "Fuck," she said, spitting the word not at him but at a world in which such things could happen. "That wasn't his leg. We have no idea where that is." Then she stepped around him and headed back to the ward.

Looking down past his and Charles' hands in the nursing home, Lester saw pants legs draped over metal stalks sunk into artificial feet resting atop two wheelchair footrests. In front of them were his own dress shoes still on the floor. Whose legs are these, he asked himself, as if it wasn't possible to say.

The handshake ritual concluded; and he forced himself to look up, turn, and go after Penny.

There she was, by the double doors that opened from the kitchen, thanking Daisy for the tomatoes. The master chef had come out, wiping her hands on her apron. After a moment, Daisy smiled and gave Penny a hug. Les could hear her say, "You are so good to help out here, honey. You can have all the tomatoes you want."

Standing with the glass in his hand, Les experienced a vision, a sudden illumination of the vast and intricate structures that brought food to the table, that nourished these bodies, that preserved their fragile place in the human community.

His mind raced backwards in time, playing a video in reverse. It returned the tomatoes in Jimmy's bowl from the table to the kitchen, pulled them out of a pot into a vacuum sealed can, packed the can onto a truck that drove backwards to a factory, crated the original fruit with dozens of others returning to the field, shrunk them to seeds planted by hand. He saw all the people who labored to prepare the soil, to tend the crop, to bring in a harvest. What a web of human hands that knit so many people together!

Even though he'd lived nearly all his life in this part of the country, his understanding of the people around him was shaped less by experience than by media successes like *Winter's Bone*, which made the region seem as lawless as the tribal regions of Afghanistan. Rather than acknowledging the rigid moral code, fierce evangelicalism, and the insistence on hard work and self-reliance of Ozark history, such *noir* depictions were created more to feed a national desire to fix degeneration within specific boundaries.

Lester knew that five decades ago, an ancient system, similarly misunderstood by nearly all Americans, had exploded in Southeast Asia. Modern arms and ideas destroyed what it had taken centuries to build up. He had been in the middle of that dissolution, but, by the grace of God, was able to leave it behind and regain his place in a familiar, functioning social structure. He had his legs, he belonged to family, he was embraced by intricate machineries of social welfare.

Remembering some words from the morning's sermon as he fell in step beside Penny, he leaned over and whispered to her, "My cup runneth over."

She was pushing Charlotte in her wheelchair, but paused to pull her head back and look at him. "Do you mean, by any chance, that you've joined the Full Plate Club?"

Aware that this could mean two different things, he hesitated. Then he said, "Perhaps you should consider it an application for membership."

~~~

Exchange

"Self Storage." Kurt Marlowe couldn't stop thinking "self storage" meant a place to park your self. Let it rest awhile. Pick that up later. Protect from loss.

Seeing that sign one more time in front of a row of what resembled connected garages on his drive to work, he thought about the moment he'd exchanged one self for another, put the old being in storage and never gotten it out again—at least not yet. That time was thirty years earlier to the day, and the place was thousands of miles from Springfield, Missouri, on the coast of the South China Sea.

Ernie Brothers, a hometown acquaintance, met him in processing and said he was taking him "shopping."

"There's a PX here?" Kurt had asked, bewildered.

"Hell, yes," Ernie asserted." Cam Rhan Bay ain't just a military facility; it's a whole damn city!"

Technically, this "PX" was a "BX," run by the Air Force, which called it a "base exchange" rather than "post exchange." But the Army rejected the rival service's lexicon for its own terminology.

Kurt was on his second day in-country, sweating in the heat and his fresh fatigues, flinching at outgoing, squinting past the perimeter to imagined snipers tunneling toward them below concertina wire.

"How many troops are here?" he wondered out loud, as if the larger that number the less his chances of becoming a casualty of war. He had never endorsed this conflict, but didn't have enough conviction to seek conscientious objector status, exaggerate a medical condition to dodge the draft, or flee to Canada.

"Twenty thousand they say." Ernie had him by the arm and was escorting him down a sand path with painted rock borders to a huge corrugated metal structure. Off-duty soldiers were filing through double doors, going in with empty hands, coming out with bags of goods. It was the essence of American consumerism reconfigured in a land that had not taken to capitalism or the principle of private property—and which would emphatically not endorse them after foreigners were ejected.

Ernie, disciple of the American way, described the life Kurt would find at this huge military base. "During the day, with mama-san and papa-san coming to work, there are twice as many people running around. We got traffic here, we got mail delivery, we got professional entertainment at the end of the day. Good buddy, you have landed at the home of the brave and the land of free, God's country."

Tired from travel, Kurt was staggering, his feet catching in the sand. A few days earlier, the last of his stateside leave before shipping out, he had been sitting after church with his fiancée on his parents' front porch is south central Missouri. Now he was on the other side of the globe. He knew he had left behind civilian clothes, the cold of winter, a familiar continent. The stale old question—"What's new?"—had been brought to life.

"I didn't think I'd need anything," he professed as Ernie ushered him inside the soldiers' general store, a vast collection of clothes, household goods, and electrical appliances stacked densely on metal shelves. His idea was that the Army would supply him with all the equipment he needed.

"Trust me, Kurt, I've been here a while, and I know. You want a fan, a lamp, a hot plate, some snacks to take to the poker games."

"I'm here to play poker?"

Kurt had been playing clarinet in the Fort Leonard Wood Army band for the last eight months, convinced that no one needed a musician in a combat zone. Then they told him on some days over the next twelve months he would be putting aside the instrument he usually carried to shoulder an M-16.

"Hell, yes, you're going to play poker. And watch movies and eat chicken grilled on the beach and dance to the best Philippino bands imitating

182

good old American rock-'n-roll your Special Services can find. 'Proud Mary keep on turnin'!" Cam Rahn Bay did have a spectacular beach where men barbecued on 50-gallon metal drums cut in half, played volleyball in the sun, and threw Frisbees—not during red alerts, of course. Half a dozen enlisted men's clubs scattered around the base featured live music and cans of beer for fifteen cents. The base chapel was rarely used.

Kurt and Ernie had barely known each other back in Fairfield; but here they were, arm in arm exchanging news from home. Who knew then they would be in the same place 10,000 miles away in Southeast Asia? But that's what the draft did: take high school classmates who never spoke and turn them into best pals in a foreign land. Off with your old self; on with a new. What would his new self be, Kurt wondered? He'd liked the old one pretty much.

The new self showed up that same night when rockets landed in the compound. At the third consecutive explosion, he realized he was not afraid. He was shocked that he was not shocked.

This was not one of those situations he'd heard about, where a man feels as if his consciousness has split off from the rest of him, a kind of impassive alter ego watching from the outside. No. He was right there inside his own body, feeling the thuds of impact on earth and hearing the slap of shrapnel hitting sandbags. He could smell explosion, see the smoke in electric lights, taste something sharp and unfamiliar in his saliva.

But his heart did not race, his stomach did no flip flops, the mind recorded what was happening and sent rational signals to the rest of him: stay down, wait for orders, see if anyone needs help. This calm was totally unexpected.

Like most boys, he'd been physically afraid many times growing up: sensing a limb give way as he climbed toward the very top of the magnificent old oak behind the Van Nostrands, seeing his father close his fist and scowl when he found the dent his bike had made on the side of the family Plymouth, backing up from Eddie "The Brute" Braxton, who said he was going to kick his ass into next week for crowding him in the school hallway. He had been sure that every day in Vietnam would be that times ten. This day was not.

Kurt had liked college because he was a good student—and it gave him a deferment for four sweet years. But he also appreciated moving into a social realm where physical conflict could much more easily be avoided than on the playground. It seemed his diploma, however, had become his greetings from Uncle Sam the day after graduation. The fistfights he soon witnessed in basic training were, he feared, a prelude to much worse.

When that worse arrived, he did not feel invulnerable, protected by some miraculous force field or the hand of God. He understood in the deepest part of his being that he could die at any moment, as others, it would turn out, were doing in the neighboring hootch . . . or what was left of it. He also knew he could be looking at a bloody stump where his arm had been, feeling his guts spill out over his bright brass belt buckle, drawing air through a sucking chest wound as he'd seen pictured in a training film.

Kurt recognized the facts of his vulnerability and his mortality as completely as he understood his parents' love for him, the beauty of the woods he had played in as a child, the power music had to move the soul. The prospect of his mutilated body was as real as the mess hall Salisbury steak he had eaten that evening or the unseasonable woolen Army blanket thrown carelessly at the end of his bunk several hours earlier.

He heard the whine of another shell on its way and thought to himself, "If the next one lands on me, I will be gone from this earth forever." But he was not upset. What would happen after his obliteration he did not know exactly, but, again, it gave him no concern. What would be would be, he thought, a principle he soon heard in his fellow soldiers' frequently uttered, "There it is."

The next day Kurt's top was told about Spec Four Marlowe's exemplary conduct and assumed it was the product of training. From those times in basic when every recruit crawls beneath horizontal lines of machine gun fire, throws a grenade with an instructor securing his grip until the moment of release, and squeezes the trigger on an automatic weapon, soldiers are conditioned to perform in combat. Marlowe must be, said SFC Johnson, someone who internalized the drill and would act under pressure by instinct, not by impulse. If only more were like him!

Ernie concluded Kurt must have lost it completely, his brain as empty as a sheep's, waking up after it was over with no memory of what had happened. Kurt, bemused, didn't bother to contradict him. But he knew both men were wrong. Had God touched him?

The way Kurt thought about it, he had done what millions of people did every day when they got in their automobiles and commuted to work on the beltway: merged with traffic racing beside them at 70 miles per hour and changed lanes to speed around an eighteen-wheeler. It was the same each fall when the homeowner cut on the natural gas furnace for the first time of the season, confident there would be no undetected leak in the basement headed for an electric spark that would destroy the house and all its inhabitants.

We live, Kurt realized, within a network of dangers contained or restrained. And we act as if survival is to be expected but not guaranteed. In civilian life, only rarely does panic break through conventional assumptions.

Even so, Kurt knew his reaction the previous night had not been intellectual. He didn't think it through or calculate the odds in his favor. He understood the possibility of being maimed, blinded, emasculated by flying debris. He just didn't get excited.

It happened twice more during his tour: at a firebase and on a convoy. And it occurred again fifteen years later back in The World: a moment when fear should have rendered him powerless but did not. The exchange of selves had not, so far at least, been reversed.

Other alterations in his nature during his time of service had not necessarily been positive. He disliked drinking as much as he did, but what could he do after a boring ten-hour shift of sandbag filling and with beer right there at the hooch? The latest *Playboy* playmate did not last long as a substitute for the very real Sharon, a natural and unaffected beauty; so he found himself too many nights on a stool at the hootch's unauthorized but permitted plywood bar. At those times, moving from civilian to military seemed to mean transition from productivity to dissipation. Well, or to misdirected industry.

Long before he arrived, the enlisted men in his outfit had worked out an impressive system of using each soldier's PX ration of three cases of beer per month to keep a ready supply close to the poker table at one end of the hooch and the television set perched on top of the refrigerator. (The Armed Forces Radio Television Service showed months-old football games and even older movies.) Kurt had his ration card punched on the 18th of every month he was in country and suspected he hefted more than his share of the 2,160 cans brought in by his company over thirty days.

Every time he went on perimeter guard duty, though, Kurt had to break the routine, exchanging his beer and his clarinet for an M-14 (not an M-16, which were reserved for combat units). And one field concert did require him to snatch the more sophisticated weapon and duck for cover.

Only a handful of 42-Rs rode the Huey west and north to Firebase Switchback that day, the small combo that would play jazz whenever they could but more often had to give up their Duke Ellington and Miles Davis favorites for the standards of the day: The Beatles "Get Back," Tyronne Davis "Can I Change My Mind," Joe South's "Walk a Mile in my Shoes." And, of course, they always closed with "We Gotta Get Out of this Place" by the Animals.

Midway through the last set, when the alto sax was gently begging, "Fly Me to the Moon," small arms fire erupted close enough for the band to stop and the audience to scramble. Kurt couldn't tell where the danger was, so just flattened himself beside his campstool and tried to read the gesture of the chopper pilot who'd flown them in. Both palms down meant he had it right.

"You gonna get you a purple heart," asserted Ernie when he saw him the next day. They were hootch mates by this time, Ernie's former bunk neighbor having taken his Freedom Bird home.

188

Kurt smiled at the small bandage on his thumb. "I scraped it deboarding back here, you moron." Then he held it up and turned his hand. "Of course, if they need to medevac me to Japan . . . a bit of R & R . . . sweet nurses taking turns pampering me . . ."

"Wait till Sharon hears you're a war hero! The whole town's going to celebrate. Probably change the name of Main Street to Marlowe Boulevard." Kurt scoffed that he was least likely in his class to be voted future warrior. Silently, he wondered, had he had a heart transplant and not noticed?

Predictably, the next letter from his fiancée was full of worry, as if she'd not understood to that point that her musician intended was part—if a marginal one—of the infantry in a combat zone. Kurt wrote immediately that he was fine and that he had not been anywhere near "the action" Ernie described for his family. She should continue to imagine him gaining professional experience in a foreign land and getting more credentials to direct a high school band. His record might even suggest managerial ability, eventually gaining him promotions and better pay.

Kurt knew there was more to it than he let on, a genuine transformation inside if nothing was different outside. And he did see more "action" six months later when the full band riding north on a convoy was ambushed. Again he had no idea where it came from, but he felt an unexpected Zen-like serenity. Unconcerned about the fate of himself as an individual, he abandoned that

189

commitment to the value of each human life so central to the culture from which he came.

In the meantime he felt more danger from pressure to join an increasingly risky money-changing scheme, a potential movement from habitual respect for authority to a willingness to play outside the rules.

"Listen," Ernie told Kurt one evening, "get Sharon to slip a $20.00 bill inside each letter she sends you. Green becomes gold over here." They were in the Chinese restaurant run by Koreans to suit American tastes in Vietnam. Kurt had been venting his anger at Lyndon Johnson, at the draft, at the rest of the country that supported a war they couldn't win. So Ernie must have assumed he'd be willing to take advantage of the situation they'd been put in.

It was illegal to introduce dollars into the country, of course, and all U.S. personnel were required to surrender cash for military payment coupons (MPC). And to buy anything off base, you had to change scrip to piaster. The black market gave a better rate than the government in that exchange, and, if you knew which Vietnamese national working on base was dealing on the side, you might get ten times the rate going dollar to piaster. With Vietnamese currency you could buy goods on the black market and ship them home for domestic sale—cameras, stereo components, jewelry. Ernie claimed to be getting rich.

"Ah, they're paying me okay," a cautious Kurt finally told him. "And they don't carry the Leblanc I want at the PX."

He already worried about the way they hired mama-sans to clean the hootch, make their beds, do laundry. Base workers would only accept cartons of American cigarettes as pay, which had become their own underground currency. When papa-sans burned human waste at less built up bases, Kurt thought of the process as dollar into food into shit into cigarette into piaster into smoke. What a cycle!

Kurt suspected goods like cigarettes purchased on the street came from the PX supply system, though at what point in the chain things dropped off the trucks he didn't know. And some soldiers bought at the PX and sold off base to get money for prostitutes or cheap booze. Those products changed Vietnamese hands a number of times before becoming someone's permanent possession.

"Ernie, you'd better be careful. You get caught and you'll end up with a different uniform back in the States."

"Ah, I'm careful, just small change. They only go after the big guys. We didn't dream up this stupid fuckin' war and we deserve to get a little extra when we can. Hey! Over here, it's a fuckin' hell hole!" Kurt understood the term "hell hole" after the ambush.

Rocket propelled grenades and AK-47 fire flew out of the jungle. The American response was swift and overwhelming. First the Armored Personnel Carrier opened up, then the bazookas and M-16s from battled hardened escort troops. It was over in less than a minute. This time, though, Kurt saw a fatal wound and injured bodies. The cries of the hurt should have disabled him, but he called out "Medic!" and knelt beside one man, telling him help was on the way, not to move. A medic was there in a second.

Afterwards, as Cobra gunships circled above them and the airwaves crackled with reports, Kurt made sure his instrument was safe, his fellow musicians under control. He, still a Spec 4, was acting like a veteran sergeant. He couldn't explain it himself.

"Don't write home about this," he urged Ernie, who, as a personnel specialist, would leave the base only to fly to Bangkok on his R&R and home at the end of his tour. He loved, though, to write of high alerts and alarming reports of enemy movement.

"Can I just say one of our convoys was attacked and not mention you?"

Kurt sighed. "I'll write tonight, tell Sharon that I don't have to go out to give field concerts any more." He insisted to his fiancée that he was so short he just played for big events and at the officers' club. And the last months of his tour did go by without incident.

Back home he married, was hired to teach in Springfield, and in little more than a decade rose to the position of principal. He knew anxiety in situations like Sharon's first pregnancy, which required an emergency Caesarian, and his mother's stroke, in the middle of a Thanksgiving dinner. But fear stayed locked away in Self Storage, even during the automobile accident.

A Volvo station wagon somersaulted the I-44 median that icy winter day and aimed its upside down tailgate at his windshield. His assistant principal was in the seat beside him, a secretary in back. Without thinking, he floored the accelerator and drove right under the flying vehicle. Jack passed out and Suzanne threw up, but Kurt pulled to a stop as quickly as he could and, finding his passengers to be all right, backed up to help the other driver.

Miraculously, the middle-aged mother of three was fine, hanging from the floor (now changed into a roof) by her seatbelt and trying to loosen the buckle. Smelling gas, he helped lower her and, with the assistance of a truck driver who had also stopped, pulled her from the car. The Volvo was justly famous, thought Kurt, for its safety record.

What structural features held him together under crisis, he did not know. Even if he hated the forces that had, years ago, generated the horrifying conditions for it, he valued the day the exchange of self had occurred. However, deep in his soul, he worried about the time he knew could arrive any day: the moment when the old Kurt came out of storage.

~~~

Tumbling Pigeons

"You're just in time," Ralph said. He took Mark by the elbow to join the crowd viewing a tall man in a cowboy hat beside a white pickup.

"What's going on?"

"Tumbling pigeons. Ever seen them?"

"Tumbling . . . ? No."

Mark had received a call from Ralph earlier in the day, inviting him to meet at the old high school in Pacific, Missouri. Ralph Banister was a local landowner and, technically, Mark's nemesis.

Mark Landon was a lead engineer for the Missouri highway department, working to secure rights for a re-routing of Interstate 44 west of St. Louis. The project was being opposed by this man, who wanted to protect a section of old Route 66 that lay on his property.

Mark knew America's Main Street had passed right through Pacific, so this meeting was probably another ploy to argue the value of TheMother Road to history. But Mark decided it wouldn't hurt to be friendly with Ralph, especially if, in the end, they had to take his house and land. He didn't realize this senior citizen would take away his comfort about history, not just in terms of highway development in Missouri, but also about what he'd done along Highway 1 in Vietnam several decades ago.

Ralph had been waiting for him on the sidewalk in front of the school, along with several dozen other people. At first Mark thought this was going to be a protest demonstration. Then he realized everyone except Ralph was facing away from him and toward the high school building (actually now converted to a condominium), watching someone in the parking lot.

Mark's mind ran through ideas of homing pigeons, messenger pigeons (he'd seen them in use in Vietnam), pigeons in the park. He'd never heard of tumbling pigeons. The man in the hat was opening wooden cages in the open cargo section of his truck. These must be the tumbling pigeons, whatever that meant.

Ralph explained. "Most people in this county think of pigeons as a nuisance. Especially in urban areas, they're always on the street pecking at food dropped by residents, or at garbage. Sometimes people feed the pigeons. You know, grandfather and granddaughter on the park bench."

"I guess I've done that myself. So, are these guys going to hop over each other, or do somersaults on the sidewalk?" Mark tried to peer around shoulders to see if the birds were jumping off the truck and onto the parking lot. But no. With a whoosh the birds, out of their cages, soared up and away in a flock. Everyone watched, some folks letting out a soft sigh or small gasp of satisfaction at the birds' flight.

Mark had heard the whoosh of wings from captured Viet Cong pigeons released by the U.S. Army in Vietnam. They had been fitted with tracking devices that would allow allied forces to locate—and destroy—enemy hideouts. Mark's engineering company's work had been delayed from clearing jungle with Rome plows until the birds could be caught and banded.

"They do their tumbling in the air," said Ralph. "You'll see."

As the birds rose up to several hundred feet and swept in an arc toward the south, out over the Meramec River, Mark realized he'd watched this many times in his youth. Most small towns, just like cities, have their resident pigeons, and they're frequently seen soaring above stores and office complexes.

Fairfield's flock roosted on the Phipps County Courthouse and could be seen getting regular exercise by flying from that hilltop location out over the town. They would sweep east out over the high school, north across the campus of South Central Missouri State College, west above the hospital, and south along the edge of Fairfield cemetery. These were the landmarks of his idyllic childhood. The pigeons freed near An Khe belonged to the pain of adulthood.

While the spectators in front of the former Pacific High School watched these birds, Ralph told Mark more. "Tumbling pigeons were first bred in the Middle East as far back as a thousand years ago. The trait is genetic, passed on, of course. And certain pigeon trainers kept tumblers or rolling pigeons as a kind of specialty."

Vaguely unsettled by this demonstration, Mark said, "It looks to me as if these birds are flying the coop."

After Special Forces released the Viet Cong's pigeons, artillery and aircraft decimated the tunnel complexes, encampments, and (perhaps) villages that were their destination. Then Mark and his fellow drivers tore up the jungle, bringing down trees, spraying Agent Orange on the remaining vegetation, blowing up any structures that might have been used to stage attacks on friendly forces and villagers.

Ralph laughed. "No, these birds aren't fleeing the coop. They do fly high and pretty far, but they'll come back across this spot a number of times. Bert Overstreet—he's the trainer—knows what he's doing." Mark could see Mr. Overstreet talking to a handful of interested persons who'd stepped up from the crowd. He gestured off in the distance to the west, shading his eyes against the bright overhead sun.

Like the sound of birds taking wing, the words "Operation Freeway" rose out of the list of unhappy missions from Mark's year of service in Southeast Asia. "Not ready for that one," he said to himself and concentrated instead on the spectacle before him.

"Why is this all happening today?" he asked Ralph. Mark still wasn't sure this wouldn't turn into a demonstration against the highway project.

"He does this about four times a year, just for fun. People in the area know about him, and word of mouth usually gets a nice crowd out for the birds. Look! Here they come."

From the east came the flock, perhaps two hundred yards up and in a fairly tight bunch. Then, all of a sudden, it appeared as if a third of them had been shot. Their wings folded up and they fell down through the main group, making it look, from where Mark stood, as if they were dozens of torn bits of papers dropped from the sky.

"Whoa!" was all he could say. And before he articulated a concern that they were goners, the tumbling pigeons unfolded their wings and flew back up to join the larger group. The same thing happened on several more passes.

"Pigeons can tumble or roll," Ralph explained. "Some do somersaults in flight, head over heels. Others dive and spin, as fast as thirteen revolutions per second."

"Wow! Why in the world do they do it?"

"We're not sure. It's genetic, as I said. Bert's explained the 'ro' gene to me, but I don't understand it completely. I thought it was some survival or escape mechanism, dodging predators. But he says it has to do with chemical processes inside the bird. They speed up the production of essential material — enzymes or something — especially important to metabolism and flight."

Mark recalled one of the few military facts he'd learned in Vietnam: the bullets of American semi-automatic weapon of that war, the M-16, would tumble, not spiral. That was not by accident, as the goal was to have the bullet rip up flesh rather than pass through it.

Again, the tumblers dropped from the formation, fluttering and flipping in brief free-falls before righting themselves. "Are they all tumblers, trading turns, or just some of them?"

"Only some. The others are a kind of base. They'll lead them home after a while."

"Oh, so he doesn't have to call them down to these cages?"

"No, they head back all on their own. When he gets there — it's about thirty miles south of here, over those hills — they'll be settled down, a happy flock at home."

As he spoke, the birds made what would be their final pass and then swung out across the Meramec. The performance was over.

"Ralph, that was great. But why did you want me to see?"

"I just thought you would enjoy it. I know you've been working hard, as I have, though we're on opposite sides of this road issue."

"I regret that, but I don't see that I have any choice. Our transportation system has to expand to handle the traffic. We need a bigger road."

"Ah, yes. But those tumblers—aren't they great! They're not just rushing along like everyone else, racing to get on with things. When they free-fall like that, I sense an unfettered joy. They drop out of the pack, but they're not really loners, not isolated beings. They have their special identity, changing the pace. And they bring the rest of us such pleasure."

"Such pleasure," thought Mark, wondering how much of that precious commodity he was finding in his professional life.

A few hours later, passing through the I-44/I-270 interchange in Sunset Hills on his way home, Mark realized he would be winding through a paperwork maze tomorrow. The cloverleaf interchange he was trying to move through might have been a model for his effort to document the case to pave Bannister's land.

The eastbound lanes of I-44 here were reduced to a single strip of asphalt on what had formerly been paved shoulder. The department was working on the old lanes to his left, and he knew this path was only temporary. But the two former lanes could not handle heavy traffic, which bottlenecked approaching an old bridge just before the interchange head of him.

As he crept along, he recalled the military's strategy for giving his engineering company breaks from difficult assignments — the fifteen-day stand-down's after forty-five days in the field. Back at the base, the men were supposed to get some distance from the operation, its dirt and grime and danger and frustration. They should return to the field with a restored sense of the mission's goals. That's when they had their occasional hootch parties where, like tumbling pigeons, they dropped out of formation and free-fell into some sort of chemically induced nirvana.

Many nights they also went to watch the Filipino rock bands that put on shows at the enlisted men's clubs. Since their music was recycled American rock-'n-roll, rhythm-and-blues, and some country and western, they were often able to disengage their brains from the daily routine. Of course, a steady flow of Falstaffs also helped them slide into relaxed, nostalgic musings of home.

The single-file row of cars Mark was following pulled onto the bridge, whose surface was also being worked on in anticipation of new damage from winter cold. They moved even more slowly across that expanse.

Of course, when bands played, soldiers always wanted the singer, if there was one, to do a striptease. As with any group back home, the

202

female lead had ways of accentuating songs with some version of a belly dance, and the male backup musicians had their synchronized steps to echo her moves. Generally, though, she wouldn't strip.

Occasionally, however, one woman, somehow knowing no one in charge that particular night cared, would respond to the room's urgency. The process usually started when a soldier close to the stage stood up between numbers and led the crowd in a chant, "Take it off, take it off!" The rest would cheer and clap, at first only halfheartedly because they expected to be disappointed. But the hope that the last restraints would slip away never left them.

Often, the instigator would pass a hat around and they'd each throw in scrip, a dollar or two. He would offer the hat to the girl, but when she reached for it, he'd pull it back and insist on clothes coming off. The rest would chant louder, pound their fists on the tables, whistle and yell, pigeons preparing to peel off from the rest of the flock.

At last Mark passed over the bridge and was back on the main highway. Traffic was gradually speeding up as it left the bumpy temporary paving and spread out onto two good lanes. He would be speeding home shortly, seeing commuter traffic bunched up coming from the other direction.

This kind of driving was frustrating, of course, and he doubted if Ralph Banister's children and grandchildren really wanted to see a return to 1950s style of travel, as represented by his section of old highway. In those days, stretches of open road had alternated with town streets that featured a stoplight at every corner. There had been no limited-access bypasses around big cities or business routes that took Sunday drivers out of the way of through traffic. You were lucky to average forty miles per hour on a long trip.

On the other hand, that way of life had more built in breaks from concentrated effort. Before fast-food drive-through chains, the length of time it took to find a restaurant, to order and be served, to look at the glass case with homemade chocolate cakes and apple pies forced you to slow down. Was it true that it's not the destination but the journey?

If the first call for a striptease captured the consciousness of the crowd of restless enlisted men and generated widespread pleading, the band's leader might signal to the other musicians. The game was on. The drummer and the bass would establish an erotic beat, and the singer would start to gyrate to that rhythm. *Boom-pa-ba-boom, boom-pa-ba-boom*. The guitar decorated the *ba-booms* with deep rich chords.

The new interstates Mark had worked on weren't built because engineers wanted something to do. Drivers demanded shorter travel time and easier driving conditions. Americans want to push the speedometer to seventy-five and not have to touch the brake pedal going from St. Louis to Kansas City, St. Louis to Joplin, Hannibal to Cape Girardeau. The days of homegrown entertainment, like tumbling pigeons, had given way to mass media headquartered in New York and California, dominating the rest of the nation.

The country's leaders back in the '50s knew from the experience of World War II that efficient transportation of weapons, military supplies, and troops made us a more powerful force in the world. Route 66 had aided the war effort because it was a sophisticated and efficient pathway for transcontinental traffic. Now it had been superseded by multi-lane, limited-access super highways with reduced grade, wide turns, high volume roads.

Of course, there were good and bad dancers on American bases in Vietnam. When the merely mechanical performed, GI's kept their focus on drinking. But they responded to singers/dancers who were subtle and controlled in the steady swing of their torsos and only occasional hip thrusts, the traditional bump and grind. The one Mark remembered most vividly, Star, danced calmly for half an hour at exactly the same pace and never removed a stitch of cloth. Yet, she brought a club full of men to a point of frenzy.

Mark noted a schoolyard on the south side of the highway and what looked like a new building under construction. Again, he was witnessing suburban growth—people moving from the city—but also newcomers from the counties further west who wanted to take advantage of the city. They came for professional sports, major shopping centers, better schools. They wanted extra commuter routes, high occupancy lanes, few toll stops in their race to activity.

The town of Pacific had lost business to faster-growing communities nearby and to the big malls on the west side of St. Louis. Mark had always liked that little town, which spread out in a flat valley among high hills. Watching the tumbling pigeons swing up and over the landscape had brought back his appreciation for a fading way of life.

The Meramec River, fed by a spring close to Fairfield and traveling toward the Mississippi, ran south of the town. Cliffs rose up on the other side of the river, and the country down that way was pretty rugged. There was one great stretch of level, straight highway, though—the old Mother Road running parallel to the Missouri Pacific tracks east toward St. Louis—that made Mark recall the innocence of childhood, the family trips before he faced the challenges of college, of war, of career.

The expression on Star's face had never varied, though she seemed to look directly at each soldier. It was probably an illusion, but Mark especially felt that she understood his needs. At times he was sure she had singled him out, her eyes locking with his through the thick cigarette haze. In a tight red miniskirt and halter top, she had — or she was! — a heavenly body.

While other band members asked if they wanted her to strip, Star stayed in one place with the microphone on a stand before her. The drummer called out to her, though the soldiers couldn't hear what he said. The bass player leered as he strummed. The guitarist pointed to the hat filling with money.

In time with the drummer's continuing beat, Star bent one knee, and the hip on the opposite side rose. She bent the other knee, and the other hip was lifted. Up and down, side to side, over and over, her pelvis rocked as men stomped their feet and groaned with the music.

Every half a minute or so, after a cycle of this gentle, regular *boom-pa-ba-boom, boom-pa-ba-boom*, Star gave her behind in its tight red miniskirt a spectacular ride. It took a semicircular journey out and around a perpendicular line running from the top of her head to a point midway between her feet. To the left her rump went, then way out back behind her, and finally around the right went this sexy woman's behind. When it returned to its starting position, Star's red bottom landed with a sweet erotic bump.

And, in a related orbit, out from their bodies traveled the confused hearts of men far from home. Aching with love for the ones they'd left behind and sore with longing inspired by a dancer from another world, their spirits revolved around the sadly fixed point of their present place in the universe. Interstellar gravity tugged them by their heartstrings, and sometimes they wept.

Mark wept, too, years later, taking the exit into Clayton where his family would welcome him home.

~~~

Reunion

I.

"In just a minute," Tim explained, "I'll be turning the floor over to Lou, who's agreed to do the storyboards."

She hadn't. Tim had interpreted her praise of what he'd done himself as volunteering to take over that part of the event. But, because his excitement about the reunion was infectious, Lou just smiled at the others and said, "Susie will help."

Susie's eyes went wide, as she realized Lou was doing to her what Tim had done to Lou. But, equally good-natured, she shrugged and turned back to listen to Tim.

"We're going to rearrange the agenda a bit, as Lou and Susie have to leave for St. Louis by 4:00." It was only 1:30, and the rest of the ad hoc committee, who were planning their 50th high school reunion, wondered what would take them so long. Tim seemed to have thought of everything already. They'd also come into Fairfield the night before, and, in an extended session at Zero's, talked, they thought, about every element of the plan.

II.

"You've already got the address list, right?" Tim had asked the group early in Friday evening. He signaled the server that they needed space for two more (Sandy and Lou had just arrived from St. Louis). Could they requisition another table to be pushed up to the two they already occupied?

"Right," agreed Mark, who'd flown into Lambert Field earlier in the day and come down in a rental car. "I've already found a program to generate the name tags from that list, which will include the old yearbook picture."

He'd done some touring of Fairfield before driving to Zero's and was pleased to find many of the old neighborhoods well maintained, the houses he and his friends had grown up in easily identifiable. The church he had had attended with his family—and then fallen away from in his college and Army years—looked in particularly good shape. Having returned to the faith in his thirties, the sight encouraged him now.

"Name tags—outstanding," said Tim. "And Laura made the reservation for the Elks Hall earlier today. I'm still on as emcee, and Parker can do the music."

Parker had a vast collection of 50s and 60s hits on his iPod and would truck a sound system in from Texas. In the old days, of course, they would have needed to hire a band or a DJ at least. But he and Tim had already sent out a group email asking for songs the class would want to hear and

210

dance to. For all the rest knew, Tim had printed up dance cards and filled out his own with members of the homecoming court.

So, wondered Mark the next day at 1:30, as the official meeting began, what was left to discuss if music, food, agenda were already set?

III.

But at the clubhouse, Tim went on as if they'd be hard pressed to get their work finished in one afternoon. "Now, since Mark has flown in from North Carolina, we also need to give him a chance to make his presentation on the reunion yearbook."

Mark smiled as Lou and Susie had. "Presentation" suggested he'd done far more in preparation than enjoy an amiable chat with his next-door neighbor, Donny, who worked at Farmtown Printers. Like the others who'd come to the planning meeting, Mark had been caught up in the unexplained rush of emotion—not all of it nostalgia—that had brought this group together more than two years before the entire class would be summoned to a two-day celebration. He had been surprised at his own eagerness and began to think it had something to do with Vietnam.

Unlike veterans of other wars—his father's in particular—he had not trained, shipped, and served in a cohesive unit "for the duration." His "Military Occupation Specialty" (MOS) did not demand the close coordination required among combat troops in the field. So, a "turtle" (slow moving replacement), he slipped in behind the desk left vacant by another information specialist who had recently boarded a freedom bird on the way out of the country.

To stage a reunion of Mark's company would have involved deciding how much overlap of time in-country between date one and date two qualified you for inclusion. As a result, there had been no such gathering, and now this peacetime civilian group, which had known each before the war but gone separate ways after, seemed to have shown up on the horizon for Mark as some sort of substitute.

"Now," Tim was saying, "one of the storyboards will be for veterans." He opened up a 36-inch high, tri-fold, black corkboard that already had Army, Navy, Marine, and Air Force insignia on it. Susie looked at Lou and nodded: again, he had already done enough that their task seemed to be claiming responsibility for it.

Charlotte Sommers said, "I was surprised to see how many of our class served in the military. When you omit the women—who, of course, were not subject to the draft—it must be nearly two thirds."

"I've got the numbers right here." Tim turned toward half a dozen canvas-covered notebooks he'd stacked at one end of the conference table. Under the table were three plastic bins full of material, the contents of which could only be guessed by the others.

Mark Lytton, who had become "yearbook editor" in the same way Lou and Sandy found themselves "storyboards artists," turned to Mike Fisher, who still lived in Fairfield, and whispered, "What doesn't this man have? He's already tracked down all but eight of our surviving 150 classmates; he's tentatively booked a place and drafted a menu with fish, chicken, beef, or vegetarian options; he's blocked off rooms for out-of-towners at three different motels."

Mark smiled. "I worry that's he arranging tuxedo and evening gown rentals and somehow bringing Lawrence Welk back to life with his entire orchestra."

Bob Justice, now the mayor of Fairfield, said, "Tim, tell the others what you're planning to recognize those who served and those who are no longer with us."

That ought to include Warren Stevens of Princeton, New Jersey, thought Mark, his hootch-mate at Long Binh—dead, buried, and mourned for forty years this spring.

"Right. I'll get that percentage in a minute," Tim told His Honor. Bob had already been asked—though he was not to tell others yet—if he could have a key to the city made for a "special guest of honor," a 1963 celebrity Tim had recruited to perform. That man was also a musical evangelist, and Tim had contacted local churches about his willingness to sing for a love offering in support of his work with ghetto education.

Tim moved his notebooks to one side of the table. "I contacted Bryce Chesterton—you all know him—played the trumpet in band. Actually, I talked to Stan Gibson, too. Were you all aware he's the mayor of Clayton now?"

They were. One of Tim's many email notices had listed classmates in the public eye. At the same time he was identifying "where we are now" (i.e. political figures, television personalities, people of significant means), Tim was also documenting "where we were then." He'd tracked down class pictures for both East and West Elementary, all four grades; found and made digital copies of junior high school newspapers; locating those of their teachers who were still living with the intention of inviting them to a special recognition. Much of this was on other storyboards Lou and Susie would have to claim, though that work, too, was already nearly complete.

"Anyway, they're both involved in 'Taps Across America.' Know about it?"

Mark did. Deaths in Iraq and Afghanistan had so exceeded official predictions that concealed loud speakers were being used to play recorded taps at military funerals. Angry musicians, using social media, created a "band" of live trumpeters calling themselves "Taps for America" who would go anywhere any time to offer tribute for those who had, as the newspapers always said, "made the ultimate sacrifice" for their country.

Lately the news kept reminding Mark of that time when he'd been the official "military escort" for a comrade and watched the family stiffen as taps were played for their son and brother. Over the years he had attended a number of services for friends and relatives that seemed more to open old wounds than to heal them. Perhaps that had been one incentive for Mark to buy an expensive last-minute ticket to Missouri: wanting to be involved in more positive experiences connecting him to the past.

Mark had thought, when Warren Stevens was put in the ground in Princeton, New Jersey, four decades ago, that he had buried his sorrow for a friend and for a divided nation. Slowly he learned it was not possible to keep those feelings hidden. And now once again recollection of that grief was battling his enjoyment of the present moment.

"So," asked Lucinda, after Tim explained what Taps Across America was. "So, Bryce or Stan will be here?" Having lived her life in Fairfield, except for her college years in Columbia, she had offered the clubhouse at her retirement complex for this meeting.

"It's better than that. They'll do what we call 'echo taps.' One will stand at one end of the Elks' large meeting room, and a second on the other. One plays the first part, the other repeats. "It's—"

They could see Tim had gotten emotional about this. Mark had as well.

"—It's very moving."

The night before there had been complete agreement that one of the goals of this weekend was not to dwell on the losses endured by the class of 1963, but to find good in the future. So, Lou spoke up bravely, "Can we have Maid Rites, too?"

They all cheered. Maid Rite was the local drive-in, still serving their famous milk shakes to all ages.

IV.

Tim had sounded the reunion note of determined optimism the night before at Zero's when he'd observed. "Just this week I discovered that Bocks School has been converted into an apartment building."

"'The times, they are a'changin,'" agreed Susie.

"It's nice that it wasn't torn down, but serves another purpose now. And there's other progress, too. Many of you already know, I think, that the old junior high school (before our time, of course, it was the old high school) is not just altered from the state we knew years ago, but gone, taken down, removed from this earth. On the other hand, there are two new middle schools, and our

216

old high school is a renovated wing of a state-of-the-art building."

Many would tour the old and the new in the morning, thanks to arrangements made by Mike, who served on the school board.

"These changes to the landscape of our past," Tim continued, "bring to mind a transition for our class some years before we even took on that identity — that is, before we reached ninth grade."

Knowing Tim, everyone settled back for a tale. Teddy signaled Betty that he needed another Jack Daniels and water, no ice. Mark began to reflect on Tim's enthusiasm for this reunion. The deliberate manner in which he was proceeding showed that he had been thinking hard about the past. What had inspired him, and then spread to the others?

"In 1958, as I recall (and correct me if I'm wrong)," Tim began, "we were the sixth grade class in Bocks School, a building which housed Fairfield's fifth and sixth grades. That combined for the first time East Elementary (where I went to grades one through four) and West Elementary (Linda Tannon's side of town,). In the middle of the year, we went to the third (the top) floor of the junior high building, a step, I now assume, necessitated by a growing county school population, a need for more space in the beginning grades."

There were nods, though Bob Justice was scratching his head as if he wasn't quite sure Tim had the details correct.

Tim continued. "This change represented for us an early introduction to early adulthood, if you know what I mean. We were suddenly walking the same halls with seventh and eighth graders and playing on very nearly the same playgrounds as high schoolers (and, oh, how grown up were they!)." The two schools were on adjacent property.

"Tim's thinking of all the girls, more mature emotionally and much more mature physically," joked Charlotte.

Mark admitted, "Hey, who could blame us poor boys kept in ignorance about sex by our repressed parents? That stuff was a mystery. We thought about 'T and A' twenty-six hours a day, but didn't know why." Then he waved at Tim. "Well, not Button, of course. He'd gotten his height already and, as I remember, stayed late into summer evenings at the Fairfield Oak playground with . . . what was her name?"

"Jenny ('Do It') Pruitt!"

Tim ignored them. "Of course, none of us had really entered into the spectacular worlds of junior and senior high school yet. Rather than moving from class to class, instructor-to-instructor, according to subject, we were still confined all day to one classroom and one teacher. But there was one specific

218

acknowledgement of our new status in a new building, one with a double meaning, as I in particular was to learn.

"You'd better tell us," said Teddy.

"Lockers, my friends, lockers."

He pulled out an enlarged photo of the third floor hall of the old school, taken from one end and tapering to the window at the other. Both sides were lined with double (high and low) lockers—lockers as far as the eye could see.

"We each had one, you remember. For the first time in our school lives, individual unique identities were recognized by a fundamental social institution."

"I see what you mean," agreed Susie. "Before that year we never had lockers, just cloakrooms." Cloakrooms were walk-in closets at the back of a classroom in which, on hooks just above (a child's) eye level, coats were hung and, on shelves just above their heads, lunch boxes were left.

Lou confirmed. "I never really thought about it, but those communal storage spaces did not distinguish each of us from the others in terms of our possessions. We and our belongings were grouped into one large community, 'Mrs. Casey's Third Grade.'"

"Exactly," Tim explained. "In the junior high school building, however, we had individual identities, and our belongings were special— valuable enough to deserve safekeeping, to be locked up. We were, at last, individuals—at least, according to the Fairfield's Public School System, the largest and most powerful social force we experienced in our daily lives."

Mark continued to listen to Tim's recollections, but he had seen in his mind's eye two more lockers: his and Warner Stevens in their Vietnam Army barracks. The hootch, like hundreds of others in that sprawling military establishment, was partitioned by crude plywood panels into perhaps twenty cubicles, each with two cots, two foot lockers, and two standard issue metal cabinets about as tall as a soldier in which personal and official items were stored.

There had, of course, been other lockers in between junior high school and Vietnam, some with heavy psychological weight. For instance, the year after they moved from Bocks School, in seventh grade, his classmates would begin taking gym. The lockers in the dank, sweaty dressing room beneath the gymnasium would represent a growing understanding of sexuality.

Puberty would have come to some but not all of the class of 1963. Undressing deep in the bowels of the building would be for some a triumph, for others an indictment. And upstairs, in the main hallway, the more innocent, public lockers would that year be haunted by their darker gym doubles, reminding Mark and his fellows of yet more powerful, and at times frightening, forces of adulthood still to be faced.

"Of course," Tim continued, "there was a less positive side to this elevation in status. If our selves deserved for the first time recognition, they also needed protection. That is, our private things had to be locked up, hidden from the dangers of this newer, more nearly adult world."

When he reached his post in Long Binh, Mark had lamented the meagerness of his personal possessions; they fit into perhaps a single cubic foot of space. Every other material thing he used was "Government Issue" (GI), his only for a specific block of time and, in a sense, loaned to him by the nation. The paraphernalia he had built or bought to insulate his inner self had been whittled away. The world was spreading into all available space, leaving him more and more narrowly confined.

"I might have assumed," said Tim, "at the time (had I been able to articulate this feeling then) that those hostile forces threatening my coat, notebooks, and lunchbox were older students, members of the rival classes of 1961 and 1962."

The round of hisses and boos was spontaneous. Mark recalled that things went missing in the Long Binh hootch from time to time, but no one knew if mama-san (who cleaned) or a fellow soldier was the villain.

"Honesty and time for reflection," said Tim, "suggest that not all our worries came from the seventh and eight grades. Some of us threatened others of us. Even more troubling, some of us proved to be our own enemies, myself included."

"Tim, you were already a B.M.O.C. You couldn't have done yourself any harm or we'd have known about it . . . and have made fun of you then and now."

"Ah, but I did. Here is how it happened."

"Whoa!" interrupted Mike. "Time for a commercial break. And get me another round will you, honey?" His wife, class of 1965, had been gamely enduring the evening. She waved him to the restroom.

While they all adjusted to this intermission, Mark thought about how storage spaces chronicle our path in this life: from a baby's tiny dresser, to an adolescent's bedroom closet, a room in your parents' home while you're at school, self-storage units for transitions, your own home's basement and attic. At every stage you put away pieces of the past, perhaps never to use them again.

When Mike sat down to his next lite beer, Tim continued. "The business of our sixth-grade lockers was at first a thrill: the private space, the lock's secret combination, the mechanical neatness of the whole operation. But joy diminished after several weeks for me when I realized how much time was being consumed in the process of taking lunch, coat, and books in and out of my own safe deposit box. This was time I could be using for play! (Did we have

222

Physical Education yet? or was it recess, as I remember?)"

"We had gym. No, wait, that was seventh grade. I think we had recess. Ah, recess!" lamented Teddy.

"Amen. Still, even with two thirty-minute recesses, a full hour for lunch, and a day that ended at 4:00, I was frustrated at lost playtime. But the solution I adopted was as predictable as its consequence."

"You ran away from school and from home, went to play in the NBA?" Tim had been the high school team's center.

"That came later," he joked. "No, I began leaving my lock in place, but not closing it fully. Then I could slide it off the handle, yank open the door, and rip my coat off its hook with dazzling speed." He paused dramatically. "Of course, the lock was stolen."

Mock "aw"'s and "ooh"'s of sympathy sounded in response.

"Of course, it was stolen! Only a child would not lock his lock, thus securing the locker. Although someone — probably from the class of 1961 or 1962 (boo, hiss!) — took advantage of this younger student, the real culprit in the loss was (even I had to admit) myself."

Mark thought back to what he had kept hidden in his Army locker: money (well, military scrip); letters from the girl he did not marry when he came home; a few items—camera, small tape recorder, cigarettes (black market currency) he'd purchased at the base PX. Really, nothing had been so valuable he couldn't survive its loss.

Warner's locker was different.

Tim went on. "How stupid, how immature to be unable to take those extra seconds to work the combination! And how I suffered with this, the lost lock. It could be replaced, I assumed, only by reporting the theft, thus revealing my own elementary school nature. I couldn't bring myself to walk into the office with a confession of immaturity, nor could I think up a plausible story that might make me look less foolish."

Mark had known from the beginning some of what Warner had kept secret in his locker, because his friend had made a point of telling him. "I want someone to know, just in case . . . " He didn't need to finish the sentence.

He went on. "Anyway, my journal, photographs, the 'if you ever receive this, I didn't make it home' letter to my folks." He had begun to "hump" with an infantry squad, gathering material for a book he would write when he came home—the true story of this war. All he carried with him—besides required military gear—were his Bible and a spiral-bound notebook.

"Every day," lamented Tim, "several times every day, in fact, I had to confront the evidence of my grade school identity. For weeks, each time I came in or went out of the building—morning,

224

recess, lunch, recess, afternoon—there stood the visible reminder of my incompetence; the lockless locker."

He held up the picture again. "Down that long alley of double lockers on both sides in the hall of adulthood, you can see it: locker, lock; locker, lock; locker, lock . . . and then the one sign of a child . . . locker, lock; locker, lock; locker, NO LOCK!"

Again there were exaggerated cries of sympathy. Tim held up a hand of protest: he didn't deserve sympathy. Then he picked up two more pictures, this time of the two seventh grade classes from Bocks School.

"I'm sure you're asking me the crucial questions: 'How did you finally solve this problem and move on? How did you manage not to be held back forever in sixth grade?'"

He waved the pictures, the class's next year.

"Well, I have to remind you of something you already know, a difficult truth confirmed by many experiences since that time. My honest answer to the lockless lock conundrum is that I do not, in fact, remember what I did to get out of this dilemma. I may have bought a replacement lock myself downtown at Ben Franklin's. Perhaps I finally confessed to my parents. Or it may be that I waited all year until locks had to be turned in and deposits reclaimed to discover that, whoops! I must have lost that lock on the way downstairs to the office."

He put up the pictures of sixth grade, then put them down, to hold again those of seventh grade. There were a lot of the same kids, but with a few newcomers and some absentees.

"But I do remember this, and it's a terrible fact of life: however I got through this crisis, by the time I had a lock again there had appeared in my world some new problem, equally awful, for which I did not yet have a solution. And, here's the worst: it's been that way ever since! Isn't it true?"

He had a sober audience more than fifty years after the event, most nodding, some holding drinks midway to their mouths.

"One of the features of adulthood," Tim concluded, "is that we are never trouble free, never without some major worry. Should we downsize and save our children later effort? Will our grandchildren make good enough grades to go to their college of choice? What supplement do I need with Medicare? And on and on and on . . . ."

As everyone sat in silent agreement, Tim suddenly brightened and said, "But then, . . . but then . . . but then we've matured, by golly! We got tough, rolled with the punches, right? New roadblocks, cross country detours, mechanical problems, and we learned to keep on moving, to become hardy survivors."

"Hear, hear!" said several.

"And buy more Maid Rites," added Lou.

And they moved on in conversation, slowly but with determination, to consider the appearance of McMansions on Harry Miller's old farm; the loss of the Pennant Hotel, Historic Route 66 landmark; the strip on Highway 00 south where WalMart, Home Depot, and Outback Steakhouse snarled traffic every evening..

Mark kept coming back in memory to Warner Stevens' empty locker.

V.

"I'll be giving the floor to Mark here in a just a minute," Tim said, thanking Lou for her "report" on storyboards. She hadn't even gotten up, but spoke from where she'd been sitting all along to say she would follow through with Tim's ideas.

Mark had realized that one of the bins under the big conference table was material for the reunion yearbook he was supposed to outline for the committee. It, too, would have already been taken care of by the tireless man in charge. Not much left now—at 4:15—but to sum up the meeting and call for adjournment.

Mark looked at his watch, and the Mayor began discretely putting papers away in a folder. When Tim had opened two of his bins to show the table favors he'd ordered, they all concluded that they had been called in as audience more than committee members. This coda to the meeting seemed unnecessary.

They had chuckled at Tim's stuffed animal toys (tigers, the high school team mascot); his coffee mugs, cold drink sleeves, note pads, and engraved pencils; the kazoos, long-sleeved T-shirts, and baseball caps with FHS prominently displayed; mini-pocket knives, cosmetic cases, and plastic jewelry; catalogs with pages turned back at yet more options.

When his display was complete, Tim observed, "Seeing the eight of you here this afternoon, and remembering the lockless locker on the third floor of the old Fairfield junior high school building, I have been inspired to rethink our past together, the life of the class of 1963. That one memory is too sad against the many warm feelings I have from our experiences years ago."

"Yeah," agreed Teddy. "Let's not dwell on it. And it is getting late . . . ."

"Agreed. In fact, I'm not only not going to let it haunt us but instead transform it to a moment of opportunity."

"Hear, hear," offered Lou, pushing her chair back from the table, anticipating—or hoping to prompt—a speedy conclusion to the day.

Somehow Mark didn't think so. This immersion in an innocent school past and the plans for a moving tribute to veterans, he decided, must be connected, an obsession it may not have been possible to untangle. He knew Tim had done two tours in Vietnam with the Navy, one off-shore and one on, before launching his own successful business. He had joined the American Legion and the Veterans of Foreign Wars, though, to stay connected with that past.

Taking the general response as encouragement, Tim proceeded. "What I've decided to do is to go back one more time to that junior high school building, using two of humanity's greatest gifts, memory and imagination. And, since you've traveled with me this far over the last two days, I invite you to come along, to revisit 1958 for an additional reunion. There is, I hope, something for you too in that building which exists now only in our minds."

They glanced around at each other, hoping one had the courage to suggest they'd had enough for one day.

"I always walked to sixth grade, so I now remember—or imagine—myself looking out the window as students from Ridgeview and other neighborhoods on the west side of town pull up in school buses. However you came then, do so now. If parents dropped you off, step out at the curb from the family car."

The others smiled: it was pleasant to recall.

"I enter through doors in the middle of the school," explained Tim, "go up one wide flight of stairs, past the nurse's station on the landing between floors, but then turn down the hall on the second floor to climb a final flight of steps at the end of the building to our, the third floor. If

229

you joined the Class of 1963 later, moving to Fairfield from another city or town, skipping (or even falling back) a grade, imagine this scene now anyway."

"We are all coming up the stairs at the same time in this memory, this imagining, so each of us will rise to the third floor first and see at once that long double row of lockers, that manifestation of our growing up, that symbol of new knowledge and experience."

Again, he had his picture to hold up.

"Instantly, we next see each other in that hall. And it's amazing how every member of the class is familiar then and now. All of us walk quickly to our own lockers. Those whose names begin with letters early in the alphabet (Cathy Agee) are at one end; others whose names start with letters nearer "z" (Cozette White) are at the other end; middling characters (Mike Lytton) fill up the space between."

In his mind's eye Mark had recreated a picture of tall, quiet Sandy Rockingham standing before her locker near one end of the hall on the second floor (the seventh grade's floor) of the junior high school building. Her hair is held back by a tight band, and she wears a soft beige sweater and a plaid skirt, knee-high socks and penny loafers.

In this fantasy Sandy has the woman's figure that blossomed unexpectedly and gloriously over the summer after her sixth grade, turning the heads of boys and men. Mark heard someone say

230

she has the male population of the junior high and half the high school "by the short hairs," but didn't know what it meant.

Her books on the floor in front of her, Sandy holds in Mark's memory/imagination her locker's lock in one hand, gently. She chews her lower lip as if she cannot remember or does not really care about the combination, about the books within, about anything having to do with formal education.

As she cups the lock in one hand, the fingers of her other hand curl to spin the knob. Her head is tilted as if her glasses might slide down her nose. She purses her lips, and a slight, airy whistle escapes them. As Mark the boy's mouth hangs open in wonder where he stands at the top of the stairs, Mark the man breathes out slowly in a decades-delayed understanding.

"And, please," says Tim, interrupting Mark fantasy. "Put a lock on my locker in this memory, will you?"

There is laughter, though it seems most have slipped away into private rather than communal visions.

Tim continues. "Bending for the bottom lockers or stretching to the top ones, Class of 1963, work the dials of your combinations, the combinations that we can suddenly now remember — two turns clockwise to 36 (for me); one back past 36 to 20; a final spin to 8."

Mark sees Sandy pull open her lock. Then he hears Warren's mother ask the undertaker to open the casket.

Tim, in what has become a hypnotic chant, tells his audience. "Locks drop down and doors swing open to reveal . . . can it be? Locked up for all these years, left behind and almost forgotten, somehow preserved and safe—our own younger selves!"

There is almost a gasp from the group.

"How open those smiles that greet us, for before them lies only a sunny world. No wrinkles frame those bright eyes because they have not yet confronted sorrow and loss. War and illness, failure and disappointment, yes, death itself has not brought down those cheeks tears that burn and scar."

Mark feels such tears. Warren had been hit by an RPG, fatal head wound. The Army classified his remains as "unviewable." But his father asked the undertaker to look; he wanted to confirm that death would have been quick. It must have been, and the undertaker had said they could see, if they wished. That's when Mark handed over Warner's "if you receive this" letter.

Tim concludes. "These eager faces can be seen, only slightly aged and strained, in the pictures of our old yearbook. So, just as I smile at these clean hopeful images on the page, we open our arms and close them around our innocence in the imagined hall of a remembered junior high school

232

building in 1958. And when we look left and right again we now see old friends and their younger selves miraculously united in the present. Around our shoulders go our arms as across time and space we sing out together, in memory and in hope, in recognition and acceptance, in self and community: 'The Class of 1963, hurrah!'"

The Concrete Boat

I.

On his sixtieth-first birthday, Arthur Waite announced to his wife, "If I'm going to learn to sail, it's now or never."

Bobbi arched an eyebrow. "Never sounds good to me."

"Hrmpph," he said, but not in anger. She was susceptible to motion sickness and would not get on any boat. If driving from Fairfield to their cottage on Lake of the Ozarks took longer than the forty-five minutes it usually did, she'd make Art sell the place.

Roberta knew, though, as her husband began his retirement, that he needed projects to prevent his drifting aimlessly from one day to the next. And there was something—something from his "other life"—he had alluded to several times over the years that made her sense taking up boating was aimed at more than occupying his time. "You are going to build it, aren't you?" she asked.

"How did you know?" In fact, he had only been toying with that idea, worrying that she would object. He could imagine her saying that it would make a mess, that he didn't have enough experience, that he would hurt himself. But now, if she was in favor . . . well, the project was officially launched!

234

In the end, her comment, which was intended to draw out and expand his retirement activity for the future, led to an unanticipated opening into the past. Art didn't admit it to himself initially, but building *The Shell* was an effort to come to terms with one of his Vietnam experiences: the sadly doomed concrete boat scheme. The scheme sank, though the boat did not.

II.

Art had first been inspired to build a boat twenty years earlier, when he learned of the death of his friend, Sam Ledbetter, proponent of the concrete boat. They had gotten to know each other in 1969 at MAC-V, the giant American base in Saigon. Art was a Mortuary Affairs Specialist then, stationed at nearby Camp Redball. Sam, a civilian contracted by the United States Agency for International Development (USAID), was helping to modernize the Vietnamese fishing industry.

"It's really like fiberglass," he had explained to Art one morning during the two-week period when he was making presentations to top military brass. Getting the support of three services and multiple agencies required repeated sessions. In between two of them, he was idling away a Sunday after attending mass. Art, looking for a place to sit while he ate free donuts at the USO, saw Sam playing chess against himself and volunteered as an opponent.

"Sooo . . . ." Art said, trying to be tactful. "So, despite the fact that the boat's made of concrete, it doesn't sink?"

"Not a bit," chuckled Sam. "You're thinking of the gangster movie cliché, where the bad guys fit the snitch with a pair of concrete boots."

Art had, in fact, momentarily pictured a man with his feet stuck in a bucket of hardened cement as two goons pushed him off a pier into the river.

Sam went on, "I probably don't need to explain Archimedes' principle to you, but it is true that a boat made of regular concrete, rather than the traditional wood, can sink if it fills with water. So, rather than add sand and rocks to the mix, we've found substances like cork that make the final product light enough to float even when full of water."

"Ah, I see." Art hoisted the last bit of pastry to his mouth. "Do you shape the boat, then, like a potter making a bowl with clay?"

"Well, you start with a wooden mould, then spread the compound on. But the great thing is you can use the same mould over and over again to raise a veritable fleet."

Art was escaping from his unit this morning and was pleased to find an intelligent and engaging person to pass the time with. Having been assigned to draft a request for more personnel and enlarged facilities at Redball (casualties were up—way up!), he wanted to put some distance between himself and his company on his one day off in the week.

Sam continued, "I use cheap, easily obtainable material. It's heavier than fiberglass, but the *Little Cormorant* will float." He opened an oversize notebook full of diagrams and handed it across the table, careful to keep it above the chess pieces and the coffee. His concrete boat had been given a boost by a significant infusion of new funds, but Sam needed complete endorsement to move forward on full scale construction and implementation.

Art inspected the drawings, which just looked like a boat to him. All the extra lines, numbers, and symbols hovering around the basic elements of the bow, the stern, the hull didn't connect parts with function. "You have a prototype?"

"It's riding the waves beautifully at the harbor in Da Nang. You ought to come see it one day."

Art laughed to himself. He had vowed not to leave the grounds of this relatively safe base again even if he received a direct order. "Well, as a mortician," he joked, "I guess I can understand vessels of some sort." He would be the third generation to run Waite Funeral Home in south central Missouri. When he had realized he was about to be drafted, he enlisted for a three-year hitch to get additional training in the field. The decision to sign up had good and bad consequences. That was the "other life" about which Bobbi knew so little.

III.

After inspecting the space in the garage of their Lake of the Ozarks house, Art asked Bobbi "You remember those plans you got me—when?—twenty years ago?"

"In the garage, O.H."

"O.H." meant "other house." They had lived in Fairfield for thirty years, but bought a small beach cottage on stilts at the Lake fifteen years ago. Over the last twelve months, they'd closed off the bottom and turned it into a garage with extra storage space. Doubling the upstairs area with a wing, they had begun the process of moving here permanently.

In this transition period, it always seemed that whatever they needed was "O.H." In fact, Art believed any item he required was immediately transported by magic from the place they were to the place they were not, including, now, plans for *The Shell*, a wide-bottomed dingy shaped on a jig made with four-by-eight sheets of plywood.

The mail order plans Bobbi had brought him long ago called for more space and time than Art had ever had, until now. And, when she gave them to him, she knew it was more a gesture toward some sorrow he was carrying from the past than an impetus to immediate construction.

IV.

"Building a boat is really pretty simple," Sam had insisted, "whether it's made of wood or fiberglass or concrete. You just need to seal everything perfectly, which is a lot easier with a compound than with wooden planks. And Vietnamese fishermen aren't going way out to sea, so the idea is to use cheaper material that lasts longer."

"The boats they use, now—they're wood?"

"Right. They've been building them the same way for hundreds of years, longer. But the country could make more money shipping the timber they're cutting down to other countries, and my boat will never wear out."

"I'm convinced, but how do you bring the locals on board? Or are you just going to manufacture the boats and give them away?"

"The goal is to teach them how to construct the boats, let them see how easy they are to use, move on to the next stage—refrigeration."

Sam explained how native fisherman would only catch enough seafood to sell and be eaten the same day. With no refrigeration, the catch spoiled quickly in this tropical climate. But America was bringing electrification to more remote parts of the country, and this could significantly raise the quality of life for many people.

V.

Two weeks after getting the unexpected go-ahead from Bobbi on the boat project, Art studied the upside-down shape that was to be covered by concrete compound. He had found *The Shell* plans in the garage of the Fairfield house (as asserted by Bobbi), bought the materials, and constructed the mould on top of sawhorses. He was actually building a boat!

Bobbi herself was "O.H" this weekend, organizing a final cleanup at their old home, graciously taken on by their church Bible study class. Their price was that the Waites come back at least two Sundays a week and keep up with their study.

"So long as the sessions are about Noah's Ark, Jonah and the whale, or Jesus helping Simon catch fish in his boat, I'll be here," Art joked.

"He'll be here," promised Bobbi.

Art thought he was keeping talk of their move from becoming too serious. He often was uncomfortable in deep discussions and used irony or humor to lighten the tone. Fortunately, most Bible class meetings were consumed with disagreement about what had happened two thousand years ago, not with what scripture demanded today. And he enjoyed the fellowship far more than the theology. The little group had been together for more than a decade, and Art found their concern for each other uplifting even if the theology was a bit thin.

240

The rector, Raymond Hellum, who sat in on but didn't direct the sessions, was particularly adept at avoiding application of Jesus' teaching, especially if it detracted from the congregation's commitment to advancing his own career. His goals for St. John's Episcopal Church were more people in church on Sunday morning, higher pledges, greater beautification of the building. Bobbi referred to him as "The Very Rev. Mr. Helium" and hoped he would be elevated as desired to some bureaucratic post at the diocese soon. Or, as she sometimes said, "O.H."

VI.

Art had been impressed immediately with Sam's concrete boat idea. Making life better also seemed an enviable job, especially when compared to what he did: bag the remains of his generation well short of their projected life expectancy; register the personal effects of lost boyfriends, sons, husbands; map exact locations of death. These were the unfortunate realities related to a military specialty of which the ultimate assignment was, respectfully, to put the fallen in the ground.

At the end of the second chess game (they had each won one), Art and Sam agreed to meet again if possible. Only when Sam turned to gather his material did Art notice the limp.

"You okay?" He paused, ready to help if needed.

"Oh, no. It's . . . this is an . . . an old injury. Doesn't seem to heal." He gestured to his right shin. "I got this when I was here before." When he lifted the leg, his foot didn't quite come up with it, the toes still touching the floor.

Art asked, "You've been working on this boat scheme for . . . years?"

"No, the boat project is new. I was with the Navy up north of Da Nang. Military advisor, technically, to a local security force."

"And . . . ?" Art wasn't going to press too hard, but Sam seemed to pause, perhaps waiting for the question.

"Ah, another time." He stretched the leg out, rubbing the thigh with his palm. "When you live with a people, you can get caught up in local life, trying to help. Now, Charley . . . well, he takes advantage of weakness, and sometimes you get hurt."

Art didn't want to know any more details. He's seen enough of them in his work. "So," he said, "you've got the number where I can be reached. Right now, with this proposal I'm doing, I can probably get away evenings. We do have a rubber match to play!"

VII.

Art enjoyed working with wood more than with the concrete, which required special clothing, was difficult to mix in large quantities, and, frankly, was not very attractive. But he felt a kind of obligation to build the boat as much as possible as Sam Ledbetter had described the process to him. Where his instructions called for fiberglass, he substituted concrete lightened with Macrolite and microspheres.

"You have read *Robinson Crusoe*, haven't you?" asked Bobbi, inspecting the inverted hull, a dozen feet long and almost five wide.

"Probably, years ago, as a child. Why?"

She was leaning on the railing of the deck, ten feet above the driveway where the boat was being built. "Well, his first attempt to get himself off the island involved chopping down a big tree and hollowing out one section of trunk to make a canoe."

"Okay."

"So, he spent a good while finding a big enough tree. This was near his inland camp, not by the shore. Then he took some weeks bringing it down with his primitive axes, and months digging out its core to shape . . . well, something like that." She gestured to *The Shell*. "Not as pretty, of course."

Art thought. "And it sank?"

"Never had a chance to stay on the surface or find the bottom. It was so far from the shore, and so heavy, Crusoe couldn't drag it to the water."

"Ah. So it had to stay 'O.H.'"

Art stepped back and looked at his vessel, which had taken more concrete than called for in the plans. He'd also expanded the dimensions proportionally in order to end up with a more stable sailboat. Mentally, he calculated the distance *The Shell* would have to travel to reach the water. He also imagined it sliding across the grass, slipping over the bulkhead, and settling permanently on the bottom in six feet of water.

VIII.

Art didn't see the concrete boat designer for about three months after their first games of chess, though they'd found ways to talk from time to time on the military phone system. Sam eventually came back to MAC-V to make his case all over again. "This time I need money for boat-building education," he explained. "Not a permanent school or anything, but I want to bring in representatives from all the provinces along the north coast and show them the process."

"So, regional officials have endorsed the idea and want others to learn?"

"Well, that's a bit optimistic. But they have approved a demonstration for those who can attend. Fliers have gone out to every village where fishing is a livelihood."

"That's great. Congratulations!"

Sam rubbed his thigh and hesitated. "I have a feeling I've missed something in all this, but I don't know what it is. We've got nobody on the ground in so many areas, it's hard to learn what they really think of us. And I can't tell what might be getting lost in translation, if you know what I mean."

"I fear that happens a lot around here." Art, disillusioned himself with efforts to improve the graves registration process, realized Sam had lost some of his enthusiasm for the boat project, as if the harder he pushed, like Sisyphus, the more weight he had to lift. He still had his one prototype but was as far as ever from sending a fleet out to sea.

"Get us another round, will you?" Sam asked, bending over to massage his shin.

Art went to the bar, but surreptitiously kept an eye on Sam. He saw him unwind a bandage on his leg that revealed a red mass of torn flesh, perhaps eight inches long. He waited until the bandage was back in place before returning.

"That leg not healing right still?" he asked, putting two beers on the table.

"Doc keeps trying different stuff. He says surgery may be needed, but . . ."

"But?"

"Well, I didn't want to tell him, but they've tried that twice before."

IX.

The image of *The Shell* on the bottom of the Lake of the Ozarks had brought back mental pictures Art had kept buried for many years—his "other life." He'd hidden them from Bobbi certainly, but to a large extent from himself as well.

While smaller units at collection points around the country generally handled recovery operations in the field, every now and then one or two from Camp Redball were sent to conduct tactical search and recovery operations of "deceased military personnel." For most of his tour, Specialist Waite's civilian experience and administrative skills made him most valuable inside Camp Redball.

Art told his C.O. after the second time he went out that he would never go again. Lt. Colonel Stone, a tactful commander, knew Art would not necessarily back up this bluff, but, aware of his value to the unit, he worked hard to avoid a showdown.

On the mission that led to his declaration, Art and Corporal Downton traveled to a rice field in the Mekong Delta. "Where are they?" Art had asked the infantry captain who'd escorted him. He was scanning the water, filled with small shoots evenly spaced in parallel rows across half an acre. Some lily pads balanced on the surface close to the edge.

"We believe they're there," said Captain Sanderson simply, waving a hand over the crop.

Art paused. "You mean . . . in the water."

"As best we can determine."

The captain went on to explain that three troops had been captured on a night patrol two weeks ago, no one could figure out how. But when the platoon counted off at the check point, they were three men short. Later a captured Viet Cong soldier confessed—under "interrogation"— that the Americans had (finally) been tied up, loaded down with rocks on their chests, and put in the water still alive.

Art thought he'd seen every kind of decomposition there was.

Too, in the past, effects of the deceased received at Camp Redball had generally been packaged separately from the remains. But in the pond near Tan An, letters from girlfriends, pictures of family, and little Bibles rose to the surface with the bodies. Despite his family history and his own considerable experience in the profession, something deep inside Art snapped.

And, finally, on the way back to the outpost they came briefly under small arms fire. No one was hurt, but the war took on a character Art had not known before.

X.

"A piano dolly?" asked Bobbi, smiling.

"It will work," argued Art, surveying the plywood ramp he'd laid out on the ground from driveway to bulkhead. "When Billy and Frank get here, the three of us can walk it down." They were from the Bible class and, some years earlier, had successfully moved the old piano from the sanctuary to the youth ministry building. True, they left some dents in the hall floor, but that damage was slight.

Bobbi had resisted telling Art he should get help—or at least advice—from some experienced boat builders. She respected his determination to get past gaps in written instructions, to parse inexact descriptions of materials, to bridge unexplained logistics. There was, she knew, more to this project than producing a boat that would float, something carried over from that "other life."

"Well, they can always pray over it," she offered, trying not to let anxiety depress herself or Art.

"Not funny."

She gambled one more time. "Or lay hands on it and spirit it over the ground?"

"Still not funny."

XI.

The last time Art saw him, he asked Sam, "The boat didn't handle well enough?" Sam was clearly discouraged, though Art couldn't quite get to all the reasons.

"Sailed beautifully," Sam explained. "Took fishermen from villages all up and down the coast of I-Corps, sailed with them downriver past China Beach, across the Bay, and out into the South China Sea. Even threw some nets over and brought up fish."

Art had slipped over to Tan Son Nhut from Camp Redball on a day after he'd had the midnight-to-8:00 a.m. shift on perimeter guard duty. Sleeping as much as he could in the morning, he had the rest of the day off.

"That sounds great. So, what was the problem?"

"The South Vietnamese. They thought it was some kind of hoax, that this wasn't the boat we were teaching them build."

In his spare time, Art had studied up on boatbuilding and understood more of what was involved. "Ah, like it was secretly make out of wood, just like theirs, but had a fake cover on it."

"Something like that, I guess. 'Other world out there, man! So, anyway, why change their own

249

methods?" He rubbed his thigh and grimaced. Art couldn't tell if was from frustration or the lingering wound in his shin.

"Well, I'm getting short, ready to turn my worries over to my turtle." A turtle was a troop's replacement, slow to arrive.

Sam concluded, "Ah, what can you do? We had them all watch the process: constructing the frames, spreading the compound, adding the fixtures. Of course, there wasn't time for them to see the boat cure through every stage, so we had to show them pieces at different points of the process."

"Sounds like it going to take more time for the concept to cure."

Art thought about how slowly the well-established U.S. military took to assess the need for more mortuary facilities, the numbers of graphs and charts to make the case, the levels of review to survive. Meanwhile, the casualties mounted. South Vietnam was an entirely different culture, and the change Sam was seeking belonged to a system of empire and colony they had resented for generations.

XII.

It was dusk at the end of a humid August day. *The Shell* floated at the side of the Waite's dock, lines securing it under a small awning and twin-eye boat fenders protecting the hull from banging against the dock during storms. In the morning, Art would rig the sail and take his first official voyage. He'd tested it without the sails in short circuits out into the creek, using the oars. But now, assuming fair winds, he'd go on to the open water of the Lake.

He heard Bobbi say softly, "Permission to come aboard, Captain." He hadn't seen or heard her come down from the house.

"Permission granted, but you're welcome just to sit on the dock, if you'd like." He was thrilled that she was here, not "O.H.": she had declined her old book club's invitation to visit for the weekend. "And it's good you've come down as dark is closing in. It's not the prettiest boat that's ever been built."

"You're right," she admitted, having observed him struggle with the rough concrete, which was hard to paint. The colors he insisted on were more appropriate for a barge than a pleasure boat. He'd also had trouble getting the wood fixtures parallel and set at even depths. "But that's not the point, is it?" she concluded.

"No, I guess you're right."

For the past two weeks, Art had taken lessons at the marina on a fourteen-foot daysailer, more maneuverable than his boat would be, though easier to flip. He would be properly cautious tomorrow, but still eager to test his new craft.

"The night's so still," Bobbi observed. She sat on the edge of the dock, her feet on the middle bench, a tote bag in one hand.

"Did you pack me a lunch?" Art joked. "I don't plan to be out that long."

"No, it's something else. I'll show you in a minute. A question, though. Are you ready to tell me why you built this boat?"

Art both admired and resented her perception. "Why, oh, you know — a new activity, retirement. We have this water . . . ." he gestured, though, as light was fading, he couldn't have been pointing to anything in particular.

"Remember when I got you the plans? You told me something about a friend who'd been in Vietnam several times. Something about boats and fishing, trying to help."

She gently rocked the boat with her feet. He heard the tree frogs starting their nightly chant.

"Yes, Sam Ledbetter. He died, you know. Took his own life, I don't know why. All I learned was from an obituary."

She waited a moment to ask. "He was depressed?"

"Probably, piecing together from the letters I got over the years . . . unfinished business, I think, though I can't know for sure." He paused. "That was a tough war, you know. We didn't finish it, couldn't finish it. And a lot of folks tried pretty hard."

She'd met Art five years after his return from Vietnam and accepted the fact that he wouldn't talk about his service, the other life. "Well, I think *The Shell* is beautiful," she asserted.

"Do you, now? You're pretty beautiful yourself."

"Thank you, Captain." She paused and then said. "I believe I will come aboard after all." She moved her feet to the center of the boat and stood easily in front of him for a moment before swinging her behind around and sitting on the bow, her feet still on the bottom.

"Hey, you did that awfully smoothly. Sure you won't take a sail with me tomorrow?"

"Positive. But I did bring something to show my respect for your work." She pulled a bottle from her tote bag. "We're out of champagne, but I thought a cold bottle of beer would suffice."

They both laughed. A tee-totaling Baptist, she didn't drink, and his tastes were not sophisticated.

She pulled two plastic cups from the bag. "First, I will christen your boat, captain, and then we'll have a toast to the fleet—boats past, present, and future."

"My goodness! You've thought of everything."

"Well, were I thirty years younger, I'd now disrobe and spread myself on the bow, a sailor's delight. But, because I'm not, I'll just drink your health and go back to the house and my book."

She took an opener, removed the cap, and poured an inch of beer in each cup. Emptying the rest of the bottle over the bow, she said softly, "I christen thee 'The Shell' and ask God for the safe return of all the crew."

"To the fleet—boats past, present, and future!" Art said. He drank his cup. After she held hers high, she handed it to him and he drank that off as well.

Then Bobbi turned toward him, light from the house illuminating her face. "Should you, Captain, after a suitable time for reflection and anticipation, wish to come up to the house, you will find me happy to see you."

He did.

~~~

Boiling Lobster on the Fourth of July

I.

The quiet riverside neighborhood of Jericho, south of Cape Girardeau, always had a block party on Independence Day. And, like everyone else, Jimmy appreciated the basics — hot dogs (though he took only the bun, not the dog), coleslaw, and beer — as well as the homemade desserts brought by his neighbors. But he couldn't pinpoint the source of the twinge of anxiety that came each year with the event.

"Something new for this year," announced his wife Nancy a week before the celebration. "We're having a crawfish boil." And the fact that crawfish, though smaller, are related to lobster brought it back: forty years earlier, the Fourth of July, a beach on the South China Sea. He feared it was going to happen again: it would be patriotism run amok *déjà vu*.

II.

Building charcoal fires in fifty-gallon drums cut in half, his unit had boiled lobster out on the beach. Someone had bartered for a ride down to Vung Tau and bought back half a dozen crates of live South China Sea lobsters. They were smaller than the New England variety and tender. The men dipped the meat in butter melted in C-ration cans on top of the grills.

Of course, there was also plenty of beer to wash them down, as the enlisted men had pooled their monthly rations over the previous weeks to build up a stockpile. And the mess hall had made enough coleslaw to . . . well, to feed an army. So everything necessary to a party was there. No one anticipated the explosion of pent up feelings that resulted. Or the other explosion.

III.

There were only about twenty homes in the small community of Jericho, most inhabited by retirees who'd grown up in the area, had plenty of money, and didn't want to take their accumulated wealth to Florida or Arizona. There was an unspoken assertion among them that, residing in the middle of the country, Jericho represented the very center of the nation.

They were, in fact, only a few hundred yards from the Mississippi River, "Father of All Waters." While their houses were not directly on the water, they did share ownership of several acres along the shore and a path, usable in most seasons, down from the low hills to a sandy beach.

Intensely nationalistic, residents put up American flags in every configuration: off a porch column slanting up and away; horizontally displayed in windows or vertically above the garage door; hoisted by rope and pulley to the top of a pole.

Jimmy and Nancy, though natives of southeast Missouri, were latecomers to Jericho and not fully accepted. Well, she was. But there was a standoffishness that many felt about him. It had recently become more palpable after his bumper sticker comments.

"I know what you mean about bumper stickers," said his next door neighbor, Dennis Jones. Both men were barbecuing on their respective patios while their wives were working in kitchens. Dennis had wandered over, martini in hand ("Shaken not stirred," or something like that). "The kids have no respect for proper language or family values."

Dennis had been a successful vice president of the local American Missouri Bank; Jimmy was a Southeast Missouri State University history professor, retired.

"Well," agreed Jimmy, "there are those with radical political agendas: 'Burn the women who won't Burn the Bra'; 'Fry Bush in Oil"; 'To Hell's Flames with Hate.' But that's just kids spouting off. They grow up, at least most of them do." He was thinking of his own son, who'd worn dreads in college but eventually became a National Public Radio executive.

Sammy clucked his tongue and took a sip of his drink. "I don't know, Jimbo." Jimmy was okay with "James" or "Jim," but had already given up on Dennis' capacity for self-examination: to him he would have to be "Jimbo." "That's where the terrorists are bred, if you ask me. They see those inflammatory statements and get the idea it's all right to blow up a school or a hospital. I say the state police ought to be allowed to inspect the cars of such hooligans."

Jimmy chuckled to himself at the out-of-date term: hooligans. "You may be overestimating their capacity for genuine action, Denny. But some of the less offensive bumper stickers still get me hot, as if a slick saying on your car is an adequate answer to the world's problems."

"Yeah, I'm with you there, Jimbo."

Jimmy knew he wasn't and thought perhaps he should just drop the topic. But, even though he took a long pull on his Sierra Nevada to stall, he couldn't stop himself. "You take some of the religious fundamentalists." He and Dennis were both Episcopalian, the largest denomination in Jericho; so he thought he might be safe with this one. "'Jesus Drops Sinners from the Cross.' Does that make any sense?"

Another sip from the martini. "Let them have their own churches, by God. The good folks attend St. Joan of Arc."

Later, Jimmy realized that's where he should have stopped. But he didn't. "It's the same with 'Support the Troops.' They think that and a yellow ribbon will save the country after 9/11. It's way too easy."

Sammy seemed to sober up a bit. "What do you mean, Jimbo? Don't you support the troops, your country?"

"Hell, yes, I do, sure. But I'm not convinced slapping a slogan on your car is enough when the world's on fire, know what I mean? Most of the folks who . . . ." Jimmy brought himself up, remembering that Dennis had used a series of deferments to avoid the draft. "Most of the folks . . . some of them are just giving lip service to the idea. They don't change their lives a bit while others . . . make the sacrifices."

Dennis studied his drink, finding it less full than he would like. "I see what you mean. Yeah, we need to support the right congressmen down there in Washington, D.C., kick some ass and make this country strong again."

Jimmy knew that only a handful of elected officials in Washington had relatives in the service. To him, that made it far too easy to go to war. Almost no one in this small neighborhood had had military experience either, despite the fact that they were the right age to have served in Southeast Asia. Jimmy thought Roger Sunn might have been in the reserves, and Nancy said Jacob Burston spoke as if he'd done time in the National Guard. But, so far as he knew, Jimmy was the sole Vietnam veteran.

He told Dennis, "Yeah. Well, look, I'm gonna' get me another beer and see to the salmon." He had stopped eating meat ten years ago, but couldn't quite give up on seafood, especially now that it was brought in even to the middle of the country so quickly. And he loved grilling vegetables from his garden.

IV.

He had not been one of the cooks at the infamous Fourth of July lobster boil and beer bash; and nobody then, including himself, would have been interested in roasted eggplant. He'd never eaten lobster and was not pleased to watch the wiggling live creatures dropped headfirst into boiling water. He was assured by the north-easterners in the group that they didn't feel a thing—death was so quick, and they had primitive nervous systems anyway.

"Hear that?" one of the cooks said to him, cocking his ear over the boiling water. Jimmy leaned closer and picked up a high-pitched sound, as if the lobsters were crying. He looked up, shocked.

But the cook laughed. "That's just gas coming through their shells, man. Sounds like a baby, though, don't it?"

"There's no pain?"

"Not unless you let them get your fingers with their pincers or spill the water on your privates!"

Jimmy was relatively new in-country and still just following the examples of those who'd been there for months. When they were off-duty, that meant watching last year's movies (*They Shoot Horses, Don't They?*) shown outdoors by mechanically plagued projectors; listening to outrageous stories of R&R sex in Bangkok (in the shower, with two girls, "Oriental" sex toys); playing poker for both scrip and Japanese-made electronic equipment purchased at low PX prices. Their duty was reassuringly routine.

A Midwesterner who'd traveled little before being drafted out of graduate school and turned into a medical supply specialist, Jimmy had spent six months at Fort Bliss, Texas, and then one day stepped out of a jet plane onto the steaming dark tarmac at Cam Rahn Bay Air Force Base. He was amazed he didn't melt on the spot.

He was pleased, though, to find himself among the same kind of men he'd served with in Texas. Some had more than a high school education, and many had enlisted to get training for civilian life. Careful not to appear superior, he was able to get respect by helping others and pleasing those in command.

He was especially happy on the day of the lobster fest that his name hadn't turned up on the guard duty roster. One of his hootch-mates, Smithfield from Virginia, begged him to take his place. "I got a hot date," he claimed. "That young slant-eye who does the laundry—young, willing, tasty. I just love her brown, sun-roasted cheeks—cheeks, get it?"

"I can't do that, man. They see your name on your uniform coming and going. And I'm not wearing yours; they stink in this heat."

"It'll be worth it. I made off like a bandit at poker Friday night when the lieutenant's flush blew up on him." In retrospect, Jimmy decided it might have been better to be on guard duty.

V.

Decades later, he had reason to believe his little talk with Dennis had circulated throughout Jericho. Nancy asked him the next weekend, "Did you say something to Dennis about war and country?" She was boiling eggs to devil for the church supper the next day. Since Jimmy avoided the meat, he could at least get protein from the eggs.

"Ah, we might have had some discussion." He was studying the clay figure of a boy and his dog he had molded, which was nearly ready to go into his firefly kiln. "Why?"

"I don't know. I came in on some conversation at the book club, after the fondue. It sounded like you'd been critical of your neighbors, their lifestyle."

"You know what I say about who fights our wars these days. I feel for the families that take up that burden while the rest of us keep going to the mall and enjoying the good life. We say we're proud of them; we give parades when they come home; but we're not willing to give up a damn thing in our comfortable lifestyle."

Nancy had heard this rant and agreed in general. But neither had found a good part to play locally in the national drama. Their last few years of work had been stressful, especially for her. She was a nurse who spent most of her career in a pediatric intensive care unit. They admitted they were retreating in the move to Jericho, but hoped to regroup and find the right volunteer opportunities after a few years of quiet.

"Like it or not, Jimmy, this is a pretty conservative community. You might try to keep your opinions more to yourself."

He muttered, "Well, I'll be damned if I'm going to be out-patriotized." He pretended he'd discovered an urgent reason to take his little figure to his shop, an outbuilding at the edge of the yard.

When he officially adopted pottery as his retirement hobby, Nancy had told him that, since he was probably going to set fire to something, his work should be done away from the main house. But that also made it a good place for him to escape. If she'd known he was researching flag kits on his laptop out there, she'd have called him back in immediately.

When he made his proposal to her, though, it seemed innocuous enough at first. "I need a sturdy flagpole, four-inch diameter butt tapering to two-inch diameter; fifteen feet exposed height; three silver anodized, seamless aluminum sections with enamel fired wall at sixteen gauge thickness; three-by-five-foot flag, nylon."

"That's all?"

"I'm pretty sure I can make the rest."

She was afraid to ask—and not to. She finally concluded it would be better to know. "The rest?"

"Yeah. I didn't want to be like everyone else, putting a flagpole in the middle of the yard or hanging Old Glory off the porch, so I've ordered a model cannon, almost full-size, in fact. It will go right at the end of the driveway. Conspicuous, you know."

"Ah, to signal the raising and lower of the colors. It's a little bit excessive, but so long as it doesn't wake up the dead."

"You know I don't like unnecessary loud noises, one of the reasons I've never cared for fireworks. No, this cannon is really a replica that doesn't make a sound. It holds the flag and the pole."

He waited for her to raise her eyebrows again. She did, so he explained. "I pull a rope at the back, see—looks like a fuse, actually—and the flag comes out of the barrel on the first section of pole."

"Oh, dear. Like the popgun in the movies, Three Stooges style. Instead of having the word 'Bang' printed on a flag, you have the Stars and Stripes?"

"Right. Then there's a neat little wheel to crank, and the other sections of the pole are jacked out to hoist the flag the rest of the way."

"If you keep this up, I might have to shoot you out of cannon and watch you drop headfirst into the river!"

He sensed she was more resigned than angry. "I want to be sure our love of country is conspicuous to our neighbors. But, listen, once it's there and everyone's seen it a few times, the gun will become background. All they'll notice is an impressive flag flying along with all the others. The cannon rocks back, by the way, so the pole goes straight up."

"Hmm. How big is this gun?"

"The, ah . . . the elevating barrel of my Napoleon cannon is five feet; the wheels on the wooden trunk carriage are 48-inches in diameter; and it comes with real rope breaching."

She would have preferred a more conventional display; but, once again, she saw the advantage of keeping him occupied with such projects. And it turned out he was right that, after a few snide comments about Jimmy's erection, the cannon seemed to have become invisible.

He deliberately chose a cannon that didn't resemble the big guns that worked day and night throughout Vietnam, churning up distant countryside, decimating enemy camps, razing jungle used for cover. The enemy's hand-carried rockets and mortars were like toys in comparison, though when one shell hit the oil truck that day, four men were burned to a crisp.

VI.

The bumper sticker and the flag episodes were bad for the Paces' standing in Jericho. But questioning the use of fireworks could have become grounds for asking them to leave.

Jimmy did it on Independence Day, too, after the large pots used to cook the crawfish had been taken off the outdoor grills and the ladies were covering the uneaten desserts. The neighbors milled around the large gazebo where they would watch the fireworks as soon as dusk was a bit deeper.

A few were still suffering tears and runny noses, as the cooks had insisted on authentically spicy pepper seasoning for the crawfish. Nancy's fingers had gotten too close to her eyes at one point, so she'd had to retreat to a nearby house and flush them with cold water.

"What do mean, something other than fireworks?" Dennis asked. "It's Fourth of July, man! We'd be the only town in the U.S. of A. not lighting up the sky in celebration of our nation's birth."

"Yeah, well, I know that, but it's expensive, right? And dangerous. Every year you read about some kid blowing off his fingers or burning down a barn. I'm saying next year we might consider alternatives."

Tim Staples asked, "What do you propose instead? We've got to have some show."

"Yeah, Jimmy, sparklers are okay for kids, but we're way past that. Balloons, confetti, a lawnmower parade?" Dennis, into this third martini, was loud enough that others, curious to know what was being talked about, were turning in their direction. Some were willing for an argument to fill up the time before the fireworks.

"Denny, this is just spur of the moment, now, but what about a dramatic performance, a patriotic play that we write and produce ourselves? The effort might stimulate our minds, get us to think not just about the beginnings of America but its future."

"Uh-oh, sounds like a lecture coming on," said Dennis, whose disapproval of academics was sometimes poorly disguised.

"Okay, now that you ask for it, I will tell a little story while we wait for the heavens to explode. I call it 'Chasing the Wild Boar into a Stew Pot,' and it will be my Fourth of July celebration." Waving his Sierra Nevada at the others, he said. "You can all listen. It's a lesson of history."

Jimmy saw Nancy give him the look that meant, "Stop right there." He couldn't help himself, though, professor that he was—and on his third beer as well.

Raising his voice, practiced at filling lecture halls, he began with a bow. "I give you Dan, prehistoric man." He pointed to himself. "He's a hunter/gather living in a cave along a hillside, right . . . right over there." He pointed dramatically to the western edge of the neighborhood behind him, where, in fact, there were several small caves. "And he has mouths to feed—a wife and children. They're all hungry."

Someone says, "Dan just needs to wait ten thousand years for the greatest crawfish boil ever!"

"Amen," agreed Jimmy as glasses and bottles were raised to toast the feast. "But Danny has only been able to catch a slow, skinny rabbit now and then, roast an occasional scrawny squirrel on a spit. And the hungrier he feels, the less strong he becomes. He needs food." There was some clucking of tongues in feigned sympathy.

Jimmy realized he had wanted this opportunity for some time, though he knew it could be his last chance—in this neighborhood at least—to get certain nagging ideas off his chest.

268

His only regret was that several of the men had already gone down to the beach to prepare the fireworks display. Still, he might have fifteen minutes before everyone turned to the east to watch the show.

So, he continued. "There is, Dan knows quite well, a wild boar living farther up the valley. He's seen him grazing in a clearing along a stream. But the animal is huge, too much for him to take on, too strong for any trap he can build. But, oh! what a supply of meat that boar would provide for Dan, Sally, and the kids, cooked in a pot over a slow fire with the right roots and herbs!"

"So, one day he thinks to himself: "There's that other guy . . . ." Jimmy hesitated, barely resisting the impulse to call him 'Denny.' "There's Billy, who lives on the other hill, across the creek. And, if he would help, together they could kill that old pig and share the bacon."

Denny chimed in. "A man, a Dan, a plan!"

"Exactly! Dan explains his plan to Billy, who's just as thin and tired and hungry as he is. Billy will flush the boar from the other side of the clearing down to where the creek winds between two large rocks, a narrow passageway. And when there's no room to turn, Dan will hop out in front of him and ram his spear into the boar's chest. From behind Billy, will jump on the impaled pig and hack away with his stone knife. They'll kill that boar."

"Ah, blood!" said Denny. "Nowadays, stories have got to have blood and sex. Is sex coming in our story, Jimbo?"

Jimmy lied. "You bet. But first, there has to be . . . there has to be . . . crime and punishment." He was wondering at first how far he would go with this story; but now, he decided, there would be no retreating. Even most of the women were staying within earshot.

"The boar drives Dan back, and Billy's first thrusts with his dagger are ineffectual. But they renew their attack, hacking and stabbing, and . . . and it is a mess! But after a ferocious struggle, they find themselves on opposite sides of their kill, kneeling and gasping from the effort."

Jimmy pantomimed the thrusting and stabbing, then dropped his arms, shoulders slumped, to represented the exhausted hunters. "Dan, panting, looks across the body of their prey at Billy, also panting, and thinks to himself, 'You know, if I didn't have Billy there, I could keep this whole thing for myself. Well, and for my family. We'd get our strength back and . . . shoot, we could take a little to Billy's family.'"

"Nice guy, that Danny," observed Dennis.

"So, suddenly, Dan jumps over the dead boar, grabs Billy by the neck, pushes him over on his back, bangs his head against some rocks, squeezes his windpipe until blood erupts from his nostrils . . . Billy's dead!"

"Whoa," said another of Jimmy's listeners. He could see several women look down at the ground. At least he had their attention.

Jimmy raised a finger. "Just about then, some sort of judge comes along. We can call her God, I suspect. And God says, 'There's a dead man here. Who's responsible for this wrong?' Dan can say, 'not me,' but there's blood on his hands, isn't there, literally and figuratively? God knows who killed Billy. And that's when the lightning bolt comes down, and all that's left of Dan is a greasy spot on the grass beside the dead boar. Phroomp!"

VII.

The image made Jimmy shiver, though he knew it was coming. He had told a variation of this story to classes many times, trying always to repress the original phroomp. Of course, few had heard that explosion because everyone who had a weapon was firing it into the air in celebration of America's independence. Even the South Vietnamese troops (ARVN) raised their M-16s to empty magazines, reload, and stay on automatic until they were out of ammunition.

"What the hell's going on?" Jimmy had asked Donaldson, the senior NCO, who, to put some control on the drinking, had moved from group to group all evening.

"Hell, sometimes it just happens. People go crazy. There's no reason for it, but it's probably about Independence Day—well, if it's about anything."

VIII.

Dennis asked, "What's the moral, there, Jimbo? This doesn't seem to connect to Fourth of July."

"Good point, but I'm getting there. I just need add a slight twist to this scenario." Jimmy saw several listeners reach to pull more beer out of the cooler, but they were not leaving. Maybe he would keep his audience to the end after all.

"So Dan and Billy, neighboring prehistoric men, make a plan to kill a wild boar for their families. Billy flushes, Dan pokes, Billy hacks, the boar is dead. The two men, exhausted, panting, kneel on opposite sides of the carcass, and Dan thinks: "You know, if I didn't have Billy there, I could keep this whole thing for myself. And for my family. We'd get our strength back and . . . well, we could take a little to Billy's family."

"So, spotting, out of the corner of his eye, a big limb fallen from a tree—a club really—he reaches over, grabs the club, beans Billy once, twice, however many times are necessary until blood gushes out of his ears. Billy's dead. Then some sort of judge comes along. And God says, 'There's a dead man here. Who's responsible for this wrong?'"

"Dan can say, 'not me, that stick did it,' and point to the club. But God's not so dumb; she knows someone held the stick; there's no one else around but Dan. There's still blood on his hands, isn't there, figuratively if not literally? Phroomp! Lightning, grease, end of story."

Even as Dennis opened his mouth to call again for the moral, Jimmy raised his hands. "Okay, okay. One more time with one more slight revision, and you get your moral." He was a bit worried about timing, as at any moment the first fizzing sound from the launch of fireworks could stop the narrative.

"Suppose, after Dan talks to Billy but before the day of the hunt, he remembers Carl, who, also hungry, lives up the creek past the boar's clearing. Dad happens to see Carl and says something like this: 'You know, Carl, you're not looking so good. Pretty thin there. The wife and kids? Um-hm, that's bad, that's too bad. By the way, I just mention this in passing, but Billy, down the way there, he and I have a little plan to kill that big boar who's out grazing in the clearing every morning. After we get him, he and I will split the meat—fifty-fifty.'"

"'Um-hm,' says Carl, interested."

"Dan, sensing Carl's eagerness, goes on. 'Between you and me, Carl, I'm not that fond of Billy, kind of self-centered, know what I mean? If something happened to him, an accident—nothing on purpose, of course!—I wouldn't feel

273

that bad, really. Say, if about the time he just finished helping me kill that boar a—oh, I don't know—maybe a great big rock were to fall on his head and splatter his brains all over the ground— well, shoot, I'd have more meat than I need, know what I mean?'"

"'I do!' agreed Carl."

"'Well, hey, I've got to run, sharpen my spear and all. Best to the family.'"

"So, you can guess what happens: Billy, panting, on his knees, gets his head bashed in and brains spread across the ground by a rock that appears to have slipped out of Carl's hands. God shows up. 'There's a dead man here. Who's responsible for this wrong?' Dan can say, 'not me, that rock . . . or someone (nodding toward Carl) did it.' But God's not so dumb; she knows someone held the rock; and she knows—well, she knows everything of course; that's the way God works—she knows that Dan paid Carl to kill Billy."

Jimmy lingered on the word *paid* and then concluded. "There's still blood on both their hands, isn't there? Phroomp!"

"That's it?" Denny was upset. "Hell, there's no moral there. Just one bad guy getting caught and paying the price."

"Why, Dennis, there is a moral. You just don't want to see it. What we've got here is the first ever voluntary military—Dan's paid killer force

274

of one, Carl. You see, 'volunteer military' is our nice word for a system that excuses us from doing the terrible things that must be done. We non-soldiers, citizens in a democracy, taxpayers, pay others to kill people in exactly the same way Dan paid Carl to reduce Billy's head to mush."

IX.

Again, the images returned from memory, and Jimmy shivered. Dumb curiosity had made him wander down to the site when the fires were dying down and the intense heat had abated. The bodies were covered with ponchos, but, as one was lifted onto a stretcher, the cover slipped off. Jimmy saw what looked like an oversized hot dog that had fallen through the grill and been left on the coals for hours.

X.

"Hey, wait a minute, Jimmy," said Staples. "Our boys are patriots. They want to serve, and they know what they're signing up for. Nobody's making them do anything for money."

Jimmy knew someone would say this, and that the answer was complicated. "They are patriots; they are my true heroes. But a lot of them join because they can't find a job where they live. Or they want to pay for their college education afterwards with the GI Bill. Or their parents know they need a little straightening out. I happen to know about this."

It was his one, slightly underhanded trick to block objections, using his veteran status. "But the fact remains, we pay them to do the bad stuff for us. And, believe me, having had to do it will cost them the rest of their lives."

There was a pause as no one had an immediate response, so Jimmy went on. "Look, there are those who would—or have—attacked this country, for whatever misguided reason. Most of us don't want to go after them, so we hire men and women to do it for us."

At the end of his little lecture now, he scanned the faces before him, seeing a look of pain on Nancy's. He couldn't tell if it came from the crawfish seasoning, what he was saying, or what he was not saying.

He sighed, holding his hands out, palms up. "My brothers and sister in Christ, there is blood on our hands on the Fourth of July."

That's when fireworks went off behind and over the heads of Jimmy's audience: exploding stars, ground bloom clusters, Roman candles, multi-break shells, Bengal fires, horsetails, spiders, crossettes, time rains. The show would go on for over half an hour.

As everyone turned around to ooh and ahh at multi-colored streaks of light, bright rising wheels, and spinning galaxies of fire, he realized

Nancy had slipped up beside him and tucked her arm under his. "Want to go home now?" she asked softly.

"No. I guess I paid for this. Might as well stay and get my money's worth."

They were quiet for a few minutes. In a brief gap between the whooshes, the bangs, and the ratta-tats-tats, Dennis began to sing "God Bless America." Perhaps half of the crowd joined in. Jimmy shrugged and picked up with "Stand beside her, and guide her, thru the night with a light from above." Nancy added her clear voice.

As the voices faded and new streaks of smoke trailed projectiles up into the night sky, she said, "You know, sweetie, all this noise and spectacle and hoo-hah may be enough for them to forget everything you told them."

"I have a feeling you're right."

He felt her head come to rest on his shoulder and the grip on his arm tighten.

Author's Epilogue: Going Away

In the summer of 1970, I walked away from my wife and her mother at the Norfolk, Virginia, airport to board a commercial flight that would take me to Seattle, Washington. I probably said something like, "I'll be back before you know it." And she may have responded that she'd write every day. Not much besides clichés will work on such occasions.

From that airport on the East Coast I travelled to Fort Lewis, Washington, and McChord Air Force Base; my eventual destination, the Republic of South Vietnam. I recall only a resigned numbness throughout that first stateside flight across the country — too much to think about, too much to not think about.

I no longer remember how long I was stuck on the West Coast, still numb, waiting for the flight out. I ate in mess halls, slept in barracks, stood in lines. With thousands of fellow soldiers, I was being processed for overseas assignment, vaguely impressed (to make a pun), that such a vast and in some ways impersonal system did, in fact, function, but also depressed at the possible results that might apply to me personally at the end.

I do recall one evening when, paperwork completed, we were told we could do as we wished. Although, throughout my brief military career, I always carried a book, I was unable to muster (another pun intended) concentration enough to take in more than a few pages at a

278

time; so I decided to check out the movie possibilities on base.

M*A*S*H, which had been released that year, was not a good choice. But the intriguing poster caught my eye and drew me into a theater. The advertisement featured a bare hand making the famous V for victory sign, a gesture which had, in those troubled times, been co-opted by the peace movement.

However, the hand, with the palm facing the viewer, was also standing on two bare, female legs, proportional to the fist as a body. (I say "female" because they sported strapless high heels.) The hand, then, was also a person.

The lower part of the palm facing the viewer, from which those legs descended, resembled someone's buttocks. The hand's first two fingers, extended upward, looked like arms raised in some kind of celebration. (A contorted version of this pose became emblematic of the conflicted Richard Nixon, who prosecuted the war at the same time he attempted to end it.) What a strange, hermaphroditic, oddly sensual figure!

Balanced on one of the poster's uplifted fingers — not the middle one, interestingly — was a soldier's helmet with chinstrap dangling loose. Was the strap about to be pulled tight for battle or the helmet to be tossed aside as no longer necessary? It was impossible to say.

The image was conflicted in other ways. With the third and fourth finger closed on the thumb,

279

the hand was beginning to make a fist, ready to fight. Yet the V for victory or peace signal meant the end of conflict. It was war and peace at the same time.

As someone sympathetic to the desire for peace, but now a willing inductee in the military, I was conflicted as well about our nation's cause. Before I was drafted. I had seen many pictures on television of anti-war protesters, lifting their hands in the peace sign. During basic training, whenever we were marching or running on or around the base, I copied the other (mostly younger) recruits in making that ambiguous gesture to passing cars, trucks, buses — V for Victory, V for peace.

M*A*S*H was a tragic/comic take on the Korean War, a conflict that in many ways foreshadowed the one I was headed to from Fort Lewis, though we have always compared the divisiveness of Vietnam with the (sometimes exaggerated) unity of World War II. In any case, I was not uplifted by the story of Hawkeye, Colonel Potter, and Hot Lips the evening before I lifted off for Southeast Asia.

My memory of the movie poster combined over the years with another theatrical image dating from the same period, though whether I saw it before or after that night on the West Coast I cannot say. In any case, the comic/tragic take on World War II, *Catch-22*, was released in 1970 also, and at some point I was struck by one graphic scene that linked itself in my mind to the hand from M*A*S*H poster.

Movie director Mike Nichols used the unsettling sequence from Joseph Heller's original novel in which a man is cut in half by a low-flying airplane. In that scene Kid Sampson is sighted at first upright on a raft with his "feet shoulder width apart" (to use an expression from military drill). A plane flying overhead hits a pocket of low pressure and dips suddenly, slicing off Sampson's head, arms, and torso. His legs, pelvis, waist wobble a second, then topple over into the water.

Sampson's male legs from Catch-22 are related to the hand's female legs from M*A*S*H, as they have no real body above them. Both sets have lost their heads, to say the least. And both are associated with military situations.

These two classic war/anti-war movies joined over the years in my memory into a single complex image that, in hindsight, seem to convey both the fractures and the bonds of our national psyche, as well as the terrible cost of war. Legs going nowhere, legs without brains, legs without hearts.

At Ft. Bragg, in Fayetteville, North Carolina, I had learned to stand on my legs at attention and at parade rest, hands behind my back, "feet shoulder length apart." However, after basic training and a year as an information specialist at Fort Campbell, Kentucky, I did not think I was combat ready and could easily conceive of myself standing unaware in the path of destruction. My head at least could be gone in (to pun once more) a split second.

Nonetheless, when the waiting at Ft. Lewis was over, I joined several hundred other men boarding military transport and leaving the realm of the familiar. We were taken first to Alaska, and I was pleased to see from the plane and the airport that magnificent landscape recognizable from movies, television, and (probably *National Geographic*) photographs. Although I could remember when, in elementary school, this would not have been the case, I was still in the United States of America. (If I'd had the Pentax camera I'd buy in the Long Binh PX later that year, I would have taken pictures.)

Next we landed on the island of Guam, thirty miles long, four wide, famous for its role in that war by which mine was to be judged. It looked less forbidding than Alaska, but it seemed to be not much more than a giant sandbar. And landing there reminded me of how small I was in the vast space of the Pacific.

Along the way to Anchorage and across the ocean I had smoked (then perfectly permissible), tried to sleep, pretended to read. I recall no extended conversations with other men, each of us alone in his thoughts, no one — so far as I was aware — traveling as part of a group to live, work, and survive together. (I sincerely hope I am wrong about this, the profound solitary nature of

282

each fellow soldier traveling to Vietnam with me. If I had to do it all over again now, I would shake hands with each one on my flight.)

In the middle of a night, confused about time (we'd crossed the International Date Line) and space ("over there" somewhere), we climbed down a moveable, metal stairway to the corrugated metal plates making a platform on the sand at Cam Rahn Bay Air Force Base. Beyond the plane, the South China Sea might have glittered in the light of perimeter towers. In the other direction would have been dark mountains rising against the stars, though I can't remember if I saw them that night or later.

Even as NCOs bellowed out orders to "fall in," the sound of jet engines and the booming of outgoing provided constant background noise. Sleep in our eyes, anxiety in our hearts, we looked for any comforting instruction. "Welcome to South Vietnam, boys. This is where the shit hits the road."

Off again to processing—this time, in-country. And my mind went back to numb. Just before that moment of self-anesthetization, however, standing at attention, I thought to myself, "If I survive this, at least I'll never have to go again." It wasn't so.

I did not go back to Vietnam physically, but I have returned—often on wobbly legs—in memory and imagination far more times than I ever expected. And like many other veterans, I remained for decades conflicted about my experience. On the one hand (to return to that motif), I believe I desired peace; on the other I can't deny I took up arms in war.

Perhaps my most unsettling returns have been in dreams. It's not that, while sleeping, I replay events from my time in Vietnam, but I find I've been sent back again, that I am once more an enlisted man in the Army, though now decades older. The scenes I imagine myself in do not involve combat; and that's not what I experienced the first time. But I'm once more an enlisted man, an Army correspondent, traveling the country researching topics or interviewing soldiers, civilians, locals.

I am, in these dreams, composed, knowing that I've done this before and that survival is possible, even probable (the numbers tell us that). Many times I am able to counsel other, younger recruits in-country for the first time. "We'll get through this," I tell them. "Just keep your head down; do what you're told; your year will be over sooner than you think." After all, I went before and came home.

I have had to accept all the comings and goings into the past by dream and memory that I believed at one time to be foolish and unnecessary. But I have, blessedly, found two consolations. The first is that these stories that mean something—to me at least—have taken shape as a result of these journeys. Fourteen of

284

them are behind you. I have no idea whether there are more in front of us.

A second thing I have gradually come to understand is that the inevitable process of reliving is true of other phases of existence, not just the times of war. We all return to happy moments in childhood, to the days we fell in love, to the years of raising children. And, as God is just and God's hand is in all things, we bring those memories forward so that they can find their places in the present.

In our end, says T. S. Eliot, is our beginning; and I have come to agree. As we travel backward and forward, over and again, now and then, I fervently pray that peace comes to us all.

About the Author

Michael Lund grew up in Rolla, Missouri, holds a PhD in literature from Emory University, and is Professor Emeritus of English at Longwood University in Virginia. He is the author of the Route 66 Novel Series, including *Growing Up on Route 66* (1999); *Route 66 to Vietnam: A Draftee's Story* (2004), and eight other novels about Route 66, all published by BeachHouse Books. Michael served in the U.S. Army, 1969-1971. For more information about Michael's other books, visit http://route66book.com/

Credits

SHORT QUOTE CREDITS

In "How to Not Tell a War Story"

—"Is That All there is?" Jerry Leiber and Mike Stoller

In "The Ugly Sweater Holiday Party,

— "Tiny Bubbles" Leon Pober

In "Writing in the Sand"

— The Carpenters' "Close to You" Burt Bacharach / Hal David

— Credence Clearwater's "I Heard it through the Grapevine" Norman Whitfield and Barrett Strong

— The Rolling Stones, "(I can't get no) Satisfaction!" Mick Jagger and Keith Richards

In "Midnight Chopper"

— "Proud Mary" John Fogerty

In "Re-up"

—"Colonel Bogey March" F. J. Ricketts

In "Exchange"

—"Proud Mary" by John Fogerty

In "Boiling Lobsters"

— "God Bless America" Irving Berlin

Route 66 books by Michael Lund

Growing Up on Route 66 — Michael Lund (2000) ISBN 1-888725-31-1 Novel evoking fond memories of what it was like to grow up alongside "America's Highway" in 20th Century Missouri. (Trade paperback) 5x8 260 pp

Route 66 Kids — Michael Lund (2002) ISBN 1-888725-70-2 Sequel to *Growing Up on Route 66*, continuing memories of what it was like to grow up alongside "America's Highway" in 20th Century Missouri. (Trade paperback) 5x8 270 pp,

A Left-hander on Route 66--Michael Lund (2003) ISBN 1-888725-88-5. Twenty years after the fact, left-hander Hugh No one appeals a wrongful conviction that detoured him from "America's Main Street" and put him in jail. But revealing the details of the past and effecting a resolution of his case mean a dramatic rearrangement of his world, including troubled relationships with three women: Linda Roy, Patty Simpson, and Karen Murphy. (Trade paperback) 5x8 270 pp

Route 66 Spring-- Michael Lund (2004) ISBN: 1-888725-98-2. The lives of four young Missourians are changed when a bottle comes to the surface of one of the state's many natural springs. Inside is a letter written by a girl a dozen years after the end of the Civil War. Lucy Rivers Johns ' epistle contains a sad story of family failure and a powerful plea for help. This message from the last century crystallizes the individual frustrations of Janet Masters, Freddy Sills, Louis Clark, and Roberta Green, another group of Route 66 kids. Their response to the past charts a bold

288

path into the future, a path inspired by the Mother Road itself. (Trade paperback) 5x8 270 pp.

Miss Route 66--Michael Lund (2004) ISBN 1-888725-96-6. In the fourth novel of Michael Lund's Route 66 Novel Series, Susan Bell tells the story of her candidacy in Fairfield, Missouri's annual beauty contest. Now married and with teenage children in St. Louis, she recounts her youthful adventure in this small town along "America's Highway." At the same time, she plans a return to Fairfield in order to right injustices she feels were done to some young contestants in the Miss Route 66 Pageant. (Trade paperback) 5 X8, 260 pp, **Audio book** on 5 CD's ISBN 1-888725-12-5

Route 66 to Vietnam Michael Lund (2004) ISBN 1-59630-000-0 This novel takes characters from earlier works in the Route 66 Novel Series farther west than Los Angeles, official destination of the famous highway, Route 66. Mark Landon and Billy Rhodes find the values they grew up on challenged by America's role in Southeast Asia. But elements of their upbringing represented by the Mother Road also sustain them in ways they could never have anticipated. . (Trade paperback) 5 X8, 270 pp,.

Audio Book on CD—Route 66 to Vietnam ISBN: 1-59630-011-6 Michael Lund's fictional commentary from the viewpoint of a draftee. by Michael Lund unabridged 6 CD's --9 hours running time

Route 66 Chapel Michael Lund (2006) ISBN 1-59630-012-4 Route 66 Chapel, Michael Lund (2006) (Trade paperback) 5 X8, 260 pp. When the forces of progress threaten the foundation of small-town life—a small church—five senior citizens, a mysterious newcomer, and one young couple band together in an unlikely campaign to save it. The embattled meeting point of old and new is Route 66 Chapel, a building curiously linked to America's "Mother Road."

Route 66 Choir-- A Comedy (2010) Michael Lund
ISBN 9781596300583   284 pp 5" x 8" In Route 66 Choir Stanley Measure takes early retirement just before September 11, 2001, and his impulsive decisions participate in an unraveling of confidence in the American way of life. His wife Felicia finds that everything she holds dear is in danger of coming apart: her marriage, her church, her business, and even her country. Who or what can orchestrate the recovery of harmony necessary to sustain the spirit of the Mother Road?

Route 66 Sweetheart (2011) ISBN 9781596300705 304pp 5"x8". This first of a novel series chronicles an American family during times of peace and war from 1915 to 2015. The first book, *Route 66 Sweetheart*, is set mostly in and around Rutherford, New Jersey, during the 1930s, where a young woman who traces her ancestry back to the early New World settlement of Nantucket comes to maturity during the Depression In the shadows of an emerging World War II.

Educators' Discount Policy
To encourage use of our books for education, educators can purchase three or more books (mixed titles) on our standard discount schedule for resellers. See **sciencehumanitiespress.com** for more detail or call Science & Humanities Press, PO Box 7151, Chesterfield MO 63006-7151   phone 1-636-394-4950

Michael Lund's five-volume novel series chronicles an American family during times of peace and war from 1915 to 2015. The first book, *Route 66 Sweetheart* (2011), is set mostly in and around Rutherford, New Jersey, during the 1930s. *Route 66 Dreamer* (2012) features the son of a Swedish immigrant who pursues his dreams of American success in Kansas and Missouri in the early 1940s. However, in both books some family members move away to distant countries and unexpected challenges.

The third volume, *Route 66 Looking-glass* (2013), will take place primarily in Missouri in 1965, but characters also travel far from home and familiar experiences. Book Four (2014) follows another generation of family members, this time from Missouri to Southeast Asia where many learn, sadly, "how to not tell a war story." In the final volume of the series (2015), the next generation travels to Europe and the Middle East to understand their identity in a multi-national community.